CROWNED AT THE DESERT KING'S COMMAND

JACKIE ASHENDEN

MILLS & BOON

First published in Great Britain 2020
by Mills & Boon, an imprint of HarperCollins*Publishers*
1 London Bridge Street, London, SE1 9GF

Large Print edition 2020

© 2020 Jackie Ashenden

ISBN: 978-0-263-08920-2

Printed and bound in Great Britain
by CPI Group (UK) Ltd, Croydon, CR0 4YY

CROWNED AT THE DESERT KING'S COMMAND

To Dr A R Coates.
So long and thanks for all the fish.

CHAPTER ONE

CHARLOTTE DEVEREAUX DIDN'T often think about her death. But when she did, she'd hoped it would be when she was very old and tucked into bed. Or maybe in a comfortable armchair, quietly slipping away over a very good book.

She hadn't imagined it would be of heatstroke and dehydration after getting lost in the desert trying to find her father.

He'd told her he was going to the top of the dune to get a better view of the dig site—nothing major. But then someone had mentioned that they hadn't seen Professor Devereaux for a while, so Charlotte had decided to go and see if she could find him.

She'd gone to the top dune where he had last been seen, only to find it empty. As all the dunes around her had been.

She hadn't been worried initially. Her father did go off on his own so he could think, and he was a very experienced and eminent archaeologist who'd been on many digs in his time. The desert was nothing out of the ordinary for him and the idea of him getting lost was unthinkable.

As her father's assistant, she wasn't entirely inexperienced herself when it came to a dig and finding her way around it, and yet somehow, when she'd turned around to go back to the site, it had vanished. Along with her sense of direction.

Again, she hadn't been worried—her father had talked a lot about how the desert could play tricks on a person's perception—so she'd strode off confidently the same way she'd come, retracing her steps, expecting to come across the site pretty much straight away.

Except she hadn't. And after about ten minutes of striding she'd realised that she'd made a mistake. A very grave one.

Of course she hadn't panicked. Panicking wouldn't help. It never did. The trick, when you got lost, was to stay calm and stay where you were.

So she had. But then the sun had got so hot— as if it were a hammer and she was the anvil. And she'd known that she was going to have to do something other than stand there otherwise she was going to die. So she'd started moving, going in the direction she'd thought the dig site would be, yet still it hadn't materialised, and now she was slowly coming to the conclusion that she was lost.

It was a bad thing to be lost in the desert.

A very bad thing.

Charlotte paused and adjusted the black and white scarf she wore wrapped around her head. She hated the thing. It was too heavy and too hot, and gritty due to the sand. It was also usually damp, because she was constantly bathed in sweat, but she wasn't sweating now and that was also a bad thing. Not sweating was a sign of heatstroke, wasn't it?

She squinted into the distance, trying to see where she was going. The sun was beating her to a pulp. A number of black dots danced in her vision. That was probably another sign of heatstroke too, because she was now starting to feel dizzy.

This was the end, wasn't it?

The rolling golden sands were endless, the violent blue of the sky a furnace she couldn't seem to climb out of. The harsh, gritty sand under her feet was starting to move around like the deck of a ship and there was a roaring in her ears.

The black dots were getting bigger and bigger, looming large, until she realised that, actually, they weren't dots in her vision. They were people, a whole group of them, dressed in black and riding…horses?

How odd. Shouldn't they be riding camels?

She took a shaky step towards them, hope flooding through her. Were they some of the assistants from the dig? Had they come to find her? Rescue her?

'Hey,' she yelled. Or at least tried to. But the sound escaped as more of a harsh whisper.

The people on horses stopped, and she must be in a bad way because it wasn't until that moment that she remembered that the assistants didn't ride horses and they certainly weren't swathed in black robes, the way these people seemed to be. Neither did they wear… Oh, goodness, they were swords, weren't they?

Her heartbeat began to speed up, and a chill was sweeping through her despite the intense heat.

Her father, who'd been managing the dig, had warned everyone about how close the site was to the borders of Ashkaraz, and how they had to be careful not to stray too far. Ashkaraz had closed its borders nearly two decades ago and the current regime did not take kindly to intruders.

There were stories of men draped in black, who didn't carry guns but swords, and of people who'd accidentally strayed over the border and never been seen again.

Rumours about Ashkaraz abounded—about how it was ruled by a tyrant who kept his people living in fear, banning all international travel both out of and into the country. All aid was refused. All diplomats and journalists turned away.

There had been one journalist reputed to have smuggled himself into Ashkaraz a couple of years back, escaping to publish a hysterical article full of terrible stories of a crushed people living under a dictator's rule. But that was it.

Basically, no one knew what went on inside the country because no one—bar that journalist, and plenty doubted that he'd even been there anyway—had ever been there and come back.

Charlotte hadn't listened much to the stories, or worried about how close to the borders they were. Mainly because she had been enjoying spending time with her father and was more interested in the archaeology they were doing than in rumours about a closed country.

Now, though, she wished she'd paid more attention. Because if the people approaching her weren't assistants from the dig, then they were people from somewhere else.

Somewhere frightening.

She squinted harder at the group on horseback. Oh, goodness, was that a…a person, slung over the back of one of their horses? It seemed to be. A person with distinctive pale hair…

Her heart constricted, recognition slamming into her. She'd recognise that hair anywhere, because her hair was exactly the same colour. It was a family trait. Which meant that the person currently slung over the back of that horse was her father.

Fear wound around her, as cold as the sun was hot. He must have got lost, like she had, and they'd picked him up. And now they'd found her too…

A tall figure in the middle of the group swung down off his horse—and it had to be a he, given that women weren't generally built like Roman gladiators—the sunlight catching the naked blade thrust through the belt that wound around his hips, and the chill that gripped Charlotte intensified.

He came towards her, moving with the fluid, athletic grace of a hunter despite his height and build and the shifting sand under his feet. She couldn't see his face, he was covered from head to foot, but as he came closer she saw his eyes.

They weren't so much brown as a dense, smoky gold. Like a tiger.

And all at once she knew that her doubts had been correct. That this was definitely not a search party come to rescue her. A group of men draped in black with swords at their hips could only mean one thing: they were Ashkaraz border guards and they were not here to rescue her. They were here to take her prisoner because she had almost certainly strayed into the wrong country.

The man came closer, looming over her, his broad figure blocking out the hammer-blow of the sun.

But even the sun wasn't as hot or as brilliant as the gold of his eyes. And they were just as relentless, just as harsh. There was no mercy in those eyes. There was no help at all.

You fool. You should have told someone where you were going. But you didn't, did you?

No, she hadn't. She'd just gone to find her father, thinking she'd only be a couple of minutes. It was true that she hadn't been paying attention to where she'd been going, as she'd so often done as a child, lost in whatever daydream had grabbed her at the time, since that had been better than listening to the screaming arguments of her parents as they'd battled each other over her head.

Even now, as an adult, she found it difficult to concentrate sometimes, when she was stressed or things were chaotic, her mind spinning off into its own fantasies, escaping reality. Though those moments of inattention didn't usually have such terrible repercussions as now, when she was left with the choice of either turning and running away from the terrible man striding towards her across the hot sand, or falling to her knees and begging for her life.

What did these guards do to people who strayed over the borders? No one knew. No one had ever escaped. She and her father were going to be taken prisoner and no one would ever hear from them again.

Running was out of the question. Not only was there nowhere to run, she couldn't leave her father. Wouldn't leave him. He'd had no one else but her since her mother had moved to the States nearly fifteen years ago—and, though he wouldn't exactly win any father-of-the-year awards, his career and all the digs he'd taken her on had instilled in her a love of history and ancient peoples that the dreamer inside her found fascinating.

She had a lot to thank him for, so she'd follow him the way she'd always followed him.

Which meant that she was going to have to throw herself on this man's mercy—if, indeed, he had any.

Fear gripped her tight, and darkness crawled at the edge of her vision. Her lips were cracked, dry as the desert sand drifting around her feet, but she fought to remain upright. She was an idiot for wandering away from the site, it was true, but she wasn't going to compound her mistake by collapsing ignominiously at this man's feet.

She would be polite and reasonable, apologise calmly, and tell him that she hadn't meant to wander into his country by mistake. That her father was a professor and she only a lowly assistant, and they hadn't meant any harm. Also, could he please not kill them, or throw them into a dungeon, or any of the rest of the things her over-active imagination kept providing for her?

A hot wind kicked at the black hem of the man's robes, making them flow around his powerful thighs as he came to a stop in front of her. He stood there so still, as if he was a mountain that had stood for millennia, as enduring and unchanging as the desert itself.

Charlotte held tight to consciousness and something about his merciless golden gaze hardened her spine, making her square her shoulders and straighten up.

She tried to get some moisture into her mouth and failed. 'I'm sorry,' she forced out. 'Do you speak English? Are you able to help me?'

The man was silent a long moment, and then he said something, his voice deep enough that she felt it in her chest, a subtle, sub-sonic vibration. But she didn't understand him. Her Arabic was rough, and the liquid sounds bore no resemblance to the minimal words she knew.

She felt very weak all of a sudden, and quite sick.

The man's golden eyes seemed to fill her entire vision, his stare hard, brutal, crushing utterly her hope of rescue and of mercy.

She would get neither from him and that was obvious.

'I'm so terribly sorry,' Charlotte whispered as the darkness gathered around her. 'But I think the man you have on that horse is my father. We're quite lost. Do you think you could possibly help us?'

Then she fainted dead away at his feet.

Tariq ibn Ishak Al Naziri, Sheikh of Ashkaraz, stared impassively at the small body of the Englishwoman collapsed on the sand in front of him.

Her father, she'd said. Well, that cleared up the question of who the man was.

They'd found him unconscious on one of the dunes. After finding him, Tariq and his border guards had then spotted the woman, and had been tracking her for a good twenty minutes. Her zigzag path and the way she'd blundered across the border straight into Ashkaraz made it clear she had no idea where she was going, though what she'd murmured just now clarified things somewhat. She'd obviously been looking for the man currently slung over Jaziri's horse.

Tariq had been hoping she'd turn around and make her way back over the border again, ensuring that she wasn't his problem any more, but she hadn't. She'd spotted them instead and had just stood there, watching him approach her as if he was her own personal saviour.

Given that she was clearly suffering from heatstroke and advanced dehydration, she wasn't far wrong.

He didn't touch her just yet, though, because you could never be too suspicious of lost foreigners wandering over his borders—as the incident with the man who'd been armed and hoping to 'free the people of Ashkaraz from tyranny' had proved only the week before. One of his border guards had been severely injured and Tariq didn't want that to happen again.

It was probably why Faisal—his father's old advisor, who'd now become his—had been unhappy about Tariq approaching this woman himself rather than letting one of his guards do it. But protecting his subjects was his purpose, and he didn't want another injury simply because one guard had been a little careless when dealing with an outsider.

Tariq knew how to deal with them; his guards generally did not.

Especially a woman. They could be the most dangerous of all.

Except this woman didn't look very dangerous right now, crumpled as she was on the sand. She was dressed in a pair of stained, loose blue trousers and a long-sleeved white shirt, with a black and white scarf wrapped around her head, which was paltry protection from the desert sun.

She did actually seem to be unconscious, but since it could be difficult to tell, and Tariq was naturally suspicious, he nudged her experimentally with the toe of his boot. Her head rolled to the side, her scarf coming loose and revealing a lock of hair pale as moonlight.

Yes, very definitely unconscious.

He frowned, studying her face. Her features were fine and regular and, though he preferred women with stronger looks, she could be said to be pretty. Currently the fine grain of her skin was flushed bright red from the heat and burned from the sun, making the pale arches of her eyebrows stand out.

English, no doubt, given the sunburn. Certainly when she'd spoken he recognised that cut-glass accent, which meant the man they'd picked up was likely English too.

He gave her another assessing look. Neither she nor the man were carrying anything, which meant their camp, or wherever they'd come from, couldn't be far away. Were they part of a tour party, perhaps? Although tour parties generally didn't come this far into the desert—they stuck to the edges, where it was cooler, safer. From where they could easily get back to the air-conditioned luxury of their hotels and away from the sun and the heat and the rumours of a closed country where men patrolled the borders wearing swords.

'Two foreigners in the same stretch of desert,' Faisal said dryly from behind him. 'This cannot be a coincidence.'

'No, it is not. She saw the man on Jaziri's horse. She said something about her father.'

'Ah…' Faisal murmured. 'Then we can safely assume she is not a threat?'

'We assume nothing.' Tariq let his gaze rove over her, scanning for any concealed weapons just to be sure. 'All outsiders are a threat, unconscious or not.'

And it was true—they were. That was why his

father had closed the borders and why Tariq had kept them closed. Outsiders were greedy, wanting what they did not have and uncaring of who they destroyed to get it.

He'd seen the effects of such destruction and he would not let it happen to his country. Not again.

There were always a few, though, who thought it fun to try and get inside Ashkaraz's famous closed borders, to get a glimpse of the kingdom, to take pictures and post them on the internet as proof of having got inside.

There were some who couldn't resist the lure.

They were always caught before they could do any damage. They were rounded up and had the fear of God put into them before being sent on their way with tales of brutality and swords—even though his soldiers never actually touched any of the people they caught. Fear was enough of a deterrent.

Though not enough of a deterrent for this woman, apparently.

'If she is a threat, she is not much of one,' Faisal observed, looking down at her. 'Perhaps she and her father are tourists? Or journalists?'

'It does not matter who they are,' Tariq said.

'We will deal with them as we have dealt with all the rest.'

Which involved a stint in the dungeons, a few threats, and then an ignominious return to the border, where they would be summarily ejected into one of their neighbouring countries and told never to return again.

'This one in particular might be difficult,' Faisal pointed out. His tone was absolutely neutral, which was a good sign that he disapproved of Tariq's decision in some way. 'She is not only a foreigner but a woman. We cannot afford to treat her the way we treat the rest.'

Irritation gathered in Tariq's gut. Unfortunately, Faisal was right. So far he'd managed to avoid any diplomatic incidents following his treatment of outsiders, but there was always a first time for everything—and, given the gender and nationality of the person concerned, Ashkaraz might indeed run into some issues.

England wouldn't be happy if one of its own was roughly treated by the Ashkaraz government—especially not a woman. Especially not a young, helpless woman. The man they might have got away with, but not her. She would draw attention, and attention was the last thing Tariq wanted.

Then there was the issue of his own government, and how certain members of it would no doubt use her as ammunition in their argument on how closed borders didn't help them remain unseen on the global stage, and how the world was moving on and if they didn't have contact with it, it would move on without them.

Tariq didn't care about the rest of the world. He cared only about his country and his subjects. And, since those two things were currently in good health, he saw no need to change his stance on reopening the borders.

His vow as Sheikh was to protect his country and its people and that was what he was going to do.

Especially when you've failed once before.

The whispered thought was insidious, a snake dripping poison, but he ignored it the way he always did.

He would not fail. Not again.

Ignoring Faisal's observation, Tariq crouched down beside the little intruder. The loose clothing she wore made it difficult to ascertain visually whether she carried weapons or not, and since he had to be certain he gave her a very brief, very impersonal pat-down.

She was small, and quite delicate, but there were definite curves beneath those clothes. There were also no weapons to speak of.

'Sire,' Faisal said again, annoyingly present. 'Are you sure that is wise?'

Tariq didn't ask what he meant. He knew. Faisal was the only one who knew about Catherine and about Tariq's response to her.

Given what that led to, he has every right to question you.

The irritation sitting in Tariq's gut tightened into anger. No, he'd excised Catherine from his soul like a surgeon cutting out a cancer, and he'd cut out every emotion associated with her too. Everything soft. Everything merciful.

There was no need for Faisal to question him, because what had happened with Catherine would never happen again. Tariq had made sure of it.

Though perhaps his advisor needed a reminder...

'Do you question me, Faisal?' Tariq asked with deceptive mildness, not looking up from the woman on the sand.

There was a silence. Then, 'No, sire.'

Faisal's voice held a slight hint of apology. Too slight.

Tariq scowled down at the woman. Obviously, given Faisal's clear doubts, he was going to have to deal with this himself.

'I can get a couple of the men to have a look around to see where she and the other foreigner have come from,' Faisal went on, perhaps hoping to assuage him. 'We could perhaps return them both with no one any the wiser?'

It would be the easiest thing to do.

But Tariq couldn't afford 'easy'. He'd instituted the law to keep the borders closed and he had to be seen to uphold it.

A king couldn't afford to be weak.

Hadn't he learned his lesson there?

You should have listened to your father.

Yes, he should. But he hadn't.

'No,' he said flatly. 'We will not be returning either of them.'

He leaned forward, gathering the woman up and rising to his feet. She was so light in his arms. It was like carrying a moonbeam. Her head rolled onto his shoulder, her cheek pressed to the rough black cotton of his robes.

Small. Like Catherine.

Something he'd thought long-dead and buried stirred inside him and he found himself looking down at her once again. Ah, but she wasn't anything like Catherine, And, anyway, that had been years ago.

He felt nothing for her any more.

He felt nothing for anyone any more.

Only his kingdom. Only his people.

Tariq lifted his gaze to Faisal's, met the other man's appraising stare head-on. 'By all means send a couple of men out to see what they can discover about where these two have come from,' he ordered coldly. 'And get in touch with the camp. We will need the chopper to be readied to take them back to Kharan.'

He didn't wait for a response, turning and making his way back to the horses and the group of soldiers waiting for him.

'Perhaps one of the men can deal with her?' Faisal suggested neutrally, trailing along behind him. 'I can—'

'I will deal with her,' Tariq interrupted with cold authority, not turning around. 'There can be no question about her treatment should the British government become involved. Which means the responsibility for her lies with me.'

There were others who remembered the bad times, when Ashkaraz had been fought over and nearly torn apart following Catherine's betrayal, and they wouldn't be so lenient with a foreign woman again.

Not that he would be lenient either. She would soon get a taste of Ashkaraz's hospitality when she was taken to the capital of Kharan. They had a facility there especially for dealing with people who'd strayed into Ashkaraz, and he was sure she wouldn't like it.

That was the whole point, after all. To frighten people so they never came back.

His men watched silently as he carried her over to his horse and put her on it, steadying her as she slumped against the animal's neck. Then he mounted behind her and pulled her back against him, tucking her into the crook of one arm while he grabbed the reins with the other.

'Continue with the patrol,' he instructed Faisal. 'I want to know where this woman comes from— and fast.'

The other man nodded, his gaze flickering again to the woman in Tariq's arms. Tariq had the strangest urge to tuck her closer against him, to hide her from the old advisor's openly speculative look.

Ridiculous. The doubts Faisal had would soon be put to rest. Tariq was a different man from the boy he'd once been. He was harder. Colder. He was a worthy heir to his father, though he knew Faisal had had his objections to Tariq inheriting the throne. Not that Faisal or the rest of the government had had a choice in the matter since his father had only had one son.

Still. He had thought Faisal's scepticism long put to rest.

It is the woman. She is the problem.

Yes, she was. Luckily, though, she would not be a problem much longer.

'You have objections?' Tariq stared hard at the older man.

Faisal only shook his head. 'None, sire.'

He was lying. Faisal always had objections. It was a good thing the older man knew that now was not the time to voice them.

'As my father's oldest friend, you have a certain amount of leeway,' Tariq warned him. It would do him good to be reminded. 'But see that you do not overreach yourself.'

Faisal's expression was impassive as he inclined his head. 'Sire.'

Dismissing him, Tariq nodded to Jaziri and a couple of the other guards in unspoken command. Then, tugging on the reins, he turned his horse around and set off back to base camp.

CHAPTER TWO

CHARLOTTE WAS HAVING a lovely dream about swimming in cool water. It flowed silkily over her skin, making her want to stretch like a cat in the sun. It moved over her body, sliding over her face, pressing softly against her lips…

There was a harsh sound from somewhere and abruptly she opened her eyes, the dream fragmenting and then crashing down around her ears.

She was not swimming in cool water.

She was lying on a narrow, hard bed in a tiny room, empty except for a bucket in the corner. A single naked bulb hung from the ceiling. The floor was cracked concrete, the walls bare stone.

It looked like a…a jail cell.

Her heartbeat began to accelerate, fear coiling inside her. What had happened? Why was she here?

Her father had wandered away from the dig site and she'd gone to find him, only to get lost in the desert. Then those men on horseback had turned up, with her father slung over the back of a horse, and there had been that other man in black robes. That powerful man with the golden eyes, watching her. Tall and broad as a mountain. He'd had a sword at his hip and his gaze had been merciless, brutal…

A shudder moved down her spine.

He must have rescued her after she'd fainted—though this wasn't exactly what she'd call a rescue. He might have saved her life, but he'd delivered her to a cell.

Slowly she let out a breath, trying to calm her racing heartbeat, and pushed herself up.

This had to be an Ashkaraz jail cell. And that man had to have been one of the feared border guards. And—oh, heavens—did they have her father here too? Had they both joined the ranks of people who'd crossed into Ashkaraz, a closed country?

And you know what happens to those people. They're never heard from again.

Charlotte moistened her suddenly dry mouth, trying to get a grip on her flailing emotions. No, she mustn't panic. Plenty of people had been heard from again—otherwise how would anyone know that the country was a tyranny run by a terrible dictator? That its people lived in poverty and ignorance and were terrorised?

Anyway, that line of thought wasn't helping. What she should be concentrating on was what she should do now.

Pushing aside thoughts of dictators and terror, she swung her legs over the side of the horrible bed and stood up. A wave of dizziness hit her, along with some nausea, but the feeling passed after a couple of moments of stillness. Her face stung, but since there was no mirror she couldn't see what the problem was. Sunburn, probably.

Slowly she moved over to the door and tried to open it, but it remained shut. Locked, obviously. Frowning, she took another look around the room. Up high near the ceiling was a small window, bright sunlight shining through it.

Maybe she could have a look and see what was out there? Get a feel for where she was? Certainly that was better than sitting around feeling afraid.

Charlotte stood there for a moment, biting her lip and thinking, then she shoved the bed underneath the window and climbed on top of it. Her fingers just scraped the ledge, not giving her nearly enough leverage to pull herself up. Annoyed, she took another look around before her gaze settled on the bucket in the corner.

Ah, that might work.

Jumping down off the bed, she went over to the bucket, picked it up and took it back to the bed. She upended it, set it down on the mattress, then climbed back onto the bed and onto the bucket. Given more height, she was able to pull herself up enough to look out of the window.

The glass was dusty and cracked, but she could see through it. However, the view was nothing but the stone wall of another building. She frowned again, trying to peer around to see if she could see anything, but couldn't.

Perhaps she could break the glass?

Yes, she could do that, and then…

A sudden thought gripped her. Carefully, she examined the window again. She was a small woman, which had proved useful on many occasions, such as in hiding from her parents when the shouting had got too bad, and maybe it could be useful now?

Or maybe you should just sit and wait to see what happens?

She could—but this wasn't just about her, was it? She had her father to consider. He might be in another jail cell somewhere or he could even be dead. Dead and she would never know.

You really will be alone then.

Cold crept through her, despite the sun outside.

No, she couldn't sit there, helpless and not knowing. She had to do something.

Decisive now, she stripped off the white shirt she was wearing—her scarf seemed to have disappeared somewhere along the line—and wrapped it around her hand. Then she hammered with her fist on the glass. After a couple of strikes against the crack already running through it, the pane shattered beautifully.

Pleased with herself, she made sure that there were no sharp shards there, waiting to cut her, and then before she could think better of it she wriggled through the window.

A large man wouldn't have made it. Even a medium-sized man would have had difficulty.

But a small woman? Easy.

She fell rather ignominiously to the ground, winding herself, and had to lie there for a couple of moments to get her breath back. The sun was incredibly hot, the air like a furnace. Definitely she was somewhere in Ashkaraz, that was for sure.

But then she was conscious of a sound. A familiar sound. Traffic. Cars and trucks on a road...horns sounding. People talking...the first few bars of a very popular pop song currently hitting the charts rising.

Puzzled, she pushed herself to her feet and found herself standing in a narrow alley between two tall stone buildings. At the mouth of the alley there appeared to be a street, with people walking past.

Despite her fear and uncertainty, an unexpected thrill of excitement caught at her.

She was in a closed country. A country no foreigner had seen for over twenty years. No one except her.

As her father's assistant she'd become interested in archaeology and history, but it had always been society and people that had fascinated her the most. Ashkaraz was reportedly a throwback to medieval times, a society where time had stood still.

And you might be the first person to see the truth of it.

Nothing was going to stop her from seeing that truth, and she eagerly started towards the mouth of the alleyway.

Nothing could have prepared her for the shock of seeing an Ashkaraz street.

Part of her had been expecting horses and carts, a medieval fantasy of a middle eastern city, with ancient souks and camels and snake charmers. But that was not what she saw.

Bright, shiny and very new cars moved in the street, beneath tall, architecturally designed buildings made of glass and steel. People bustled along on the footpaths, some robed, some in the kind of clothes she would have seen on the streets in London. In amongst the glass and steel were historic buildings, beautifully preserved, and shops and cafés lined the streets. People were sitting at tables outside, talking, laughing, working, looking at their smartphones.

There was an energy to the place, which was clearly a bustling, successful, prosperous city.

Definitely not the poverty-stricken nation with a beaten-down populace crushed under the thumb of a dictator that the rest of the world thought it to be.

What on earth was going on?

Amazed, Charlotte stepped out onto the footpath, joining the stream of people walking along it, oblivious to the glances she was receiving.

There was a beautiful park up ahead, with a fountain and lush gardens, lots of benches to sit on and a playground for children. Already there seemed to be a number of kids there, screaming and laughing while their indulgent parents looked on.

This was…incredible. Amazing. How was this even possible? Was this the truth that Ashkaraz had been hiding all along?

She was so busy staring that she didn't notice the uniformed man coming up behind her until his fingers wrapped around her arm. And then a long black car pulled up to the kerb and Charlotte found herself bundled into the back of it.

She opened her mouth to protest, but there wasn't even time for her to scream. Something black and suffocating was put over her head and the car started moving.

The fingers around her arm were firm—not hurting, but definitely ensuring that she couldn't get away. Fear, coming a little late to the party, suddenly rose up inside her, choking.

Did you really think you could escape from that jail cell and start wandering around like nothing was wrong?

She hadn't been thinking—that was the problem. She'd got out of that cell and then been caught up in the wonder of the city outside it.

Charlotte slumped back in the seat, trying not to panic. Now, not only was her chance to escape gone but so was her father's.

And it was all her fault.

The car drove for what seemed like ages and then slowed to a stop. She was pulled out of it and then taken up some steps. Sun and heat surrounded her for a second, and then she must have been taken inside because the sun had disappeared, to be replaced by blessedly cool air. Her footsteps echoed on a tiled floor, and there was the scent of water and flowers in the air.

She couldn't see a thing through the black fabric around her head, and her sense of direction was soon gone as she was pulled down more corridors, around corners, and up yet more stairs.

Were they taking her back to that cell? Or were there worse things in store for her? Would they perhaps murder her? Make her disappear? Hold her prisoner for ever?

She was just starting to be very, very afraid when she was pulled to a stop and the fabric covering her head was abruptly tugged off.

Charlotte blinked in the bright light.

She appeared to be standing in a large room lined with shelves, containing lots of books and folders and filing boxes. The exquisite tiled floor was covered in thick, brightly coloured silk rugs, the walls also tiled, in silvery, slightly iridescent tiles. There was a window in front of her that gave a view onto a beautiful garden, where a fountain played amongst palms and other shrubs, as well as many different kinds of flowers.

A huge, heavy desk made of time-blackened wood stood before the window. The polished surface was clean of everything except a sleek-looking computer monitor and keyboard, and a small, elegant silver vase with a spray of fresh jasmine in it.

This was certainly *not* a jail cell. In fact, it looked like someone's office…

She blinked again and turned around to see two men stationed on either side of the double doors. They were dressed in black robes with swords on their hips, their faces absolutely impassive.

She would have thought the robes and swords only ceremonial, except they didn't have the clean and pressed look she would have expected. The fabric of their robes was dusty and stained around the hems, as were the boots the men wore. And although the edges of the swords were bright, was that…blood she could see on the steel? Surely it couldn't be.

Charlotte stared, her heartbeat getting faster and faster, and then suddenly from behind her came the sound of a door opening and closing.

She turned back sharply to see that a man had come into the room from a door off to her left, and he was now standing beside the desk, staring at her.

He was very, very tall and very, very broad, built more like an ancient warrior than a businessman. The muscles of his chest and arms were straining the white cotton of his business shirt, and the dark wool of his suit trousers pulled tight around his powerful thighs.

His face was a harsh composition of planes and angles that nevertheless managed to be utterly compelling, with high cheekbones and an aquiline nose, straight black brows and a beautifully carved mouth.

'Handsome' was far too bland a word for him…especially as he radiated the kind of arrogant charisma reserved only for the very powerful and very important.

But that wasn't what held Charlotte absolutely rooted to the spot.

It was his eyes. Burning gold, with the same relentless, brutal heat as the desert sun.

It was the man who'd approached her in the desert. She was sure of it. She'd never forget those eyes.

He said nothing for a long moment and neither did Charlotte, since she couldn't seem to find her voice. Then his gaze shifted to the men behind her and he gave a slight tilt of his head. A couple of seconds later she heard the door shut behind her, the men clearly having obeyed some unspoken order and left.

The room abruptly felt tiny and cramped, the space too small to accommodate both her and the man in front of her. Or maybe he seemed to get larger and more intimidating, taking up all the air and leaving none for her.

She lifted her chin, trying to get her heartbeat under control at the same time as trying to hold his relentless gaze, but she couldn't seem to manage both—especially not when he moved suddenly, coming over to the desk and standing in front of it, folding his arms across his massive chest.

Bringing him quite a bit closer.

She resisted the urge to take a step back, hating how small and insignificant his sheer size made her feel. It was exactly the same feeling that had filled her when her parents had argued and she'd hidden under the dining room table. They'd never noticed that she'd left her seat—which was ironic, since more often than not they had been shouting about her.

Clasping her hands in front of her to prevent them from shaking, Charlotte took a small, silent breath. 'Um…do you speak English?' Her voice sounded thin and reedy in the silence of the room.

The man said nothing, continuing to stare at her.

It was extremely unnerving.

Her mouth had dried and she wished her Arabic was better. Because maybe he didn't understand English. She wanted to ask him where her father was and also to thank him for saving her.

He put you in a cell, remember?

Sure, but maybe that hadn't been him. He might look like a medieval warrior, but the suit he was wearing was thoroughly modern. Perhaps he was an accountant? Or the chief of the jail she'd been put in? Or a government functionary?

Yet none of those things seemed to fit. He was too magnetic, too charismatic to be any-one's mere functionary. No, this man had an aura about him that spoke of command, as if he ex-pected everyone to fall to their knees around him.

Sadly for him, she wouldn't be falling any-where in front of him.

Except you already have. In the desert.

That, alas, was true.

'I'm s-sorry,' she stuttered, casting around for something to say. 'I should have thanked you for saving my life. But can you tell me where my father is? We got lost, you see. And I... I...' She faltered, all her words crushed by the weight of his stare.

This was silly. Her father could be dead or in a jail cell and she was letting this man get to her. She couldn't get pathetic now.

Perhaps introducing herself would help. After all, she'd had no identification on her when she'd collapsed, so maybe they had no idea who she or her father were. Maybe that was why she had been put in the cell? Maybe they thought she was some kind of insurgent, hoping to…?

But, no. Best not get carried away. Keep thinking in the here and now.

'So,' Charlotte said, pulling herself together. 'My name is—'

'Charlotte Devereaux,' the man interrupted in a deep, slightly rough voice. 'You are an assistant attached to an archaeological dig that your father, Professor Martin Devereaux is managing in conjunction with the University of Siddq.'

His English was perfect, his accent almost imperceptible.

'You both come from Cornwall, but you live in London and at present are employed by your father's university as his assistant. You are twenty-three years old, have no dependents, and live in a flat with a couple of friends in Clapham.'

Charlotte could feel her mouth hanging open in shock. How did he know all this stuff? How had he found out?

'I…' she began.

But he hadn't finished, because he was going on, ignoring her entirely, 'Can you tell me, please, what you were doing out there in the desert? Neither you nor your father were anywhere near your dig site. In fact, that is the whole reason you are here. You crossed the border into Ashkaraz—you do understand that, do you not?'

She flushed at the note of condescension in his voice, but took heart from the fact that he was talking of her father in the present tense.

'Are you saying that my father is alive?' she asked, needing to be sure.

'Yes,' the man said flatly. 'He is alive.'

Relief filled her, making her breath catch. 'Oh, I'm so glad. He wandered away from the site, the way he sometimes does, and I went to try and find him. I walked up a dune and somehow—'

'I am not interested in how you got lost, Miss Devereaux,' the man interrupted, his voice like iron, his golden stare pitiless. 'What I am interested in is how you somehow got out of a secure facility.'

Charlotte swallowed. Briefly she debated lying, but since she was in a lot of trouble already there was no point in making it any worse.

'I...smashed the glass and crawled out of the window.' She lifted her chin a little to show him that she wouldn't be cowed. 'It really wasn't that difficult.'

'You crawled out of the window?' he repeated,

his voice flat, the lines of his brutally handsome face set and hard. 'And what made you think that was a good idea?'

'I've heard the rumours,' she said defensively. 'About how people who stray over your borders disappear for ever, never to be seen again. How they're beaten and terrorised. And I didn't know what had happened to my father.' She steeled herself. 'I saw an opportunity to escape, to see if I could find him, and so I took it.'

The man said nothing, but that stare of his felt like a weight pressing her down and crushing her into dust.

You're really for it now.

Charlotte gripped her hands together, lifted her chin another inch and stared back. 'We're British citizens, you know. You can't just make us disappear like all the rest. My dad is a very well-respected academic. Once people realise we're missing they'll send others to find us. So you'd better tell whoever is in charge here that—'

'No need. All the interested parties already know.'

'Which interested parties?'

His face was impassive. 'Me.'

'You?' Charlotte tried to look sceptical and failed. 'And who exactly are you?'

'I am the one in charge,' he said, without any emphasis at all.

'Oh? Are you the head of the police or something?'

It would explain his aura of command, after all.

'No. I am not the head of the police.'

His eyes gleamed with something that made her breath catch.

'I am the head of the country. I am the Sheikh of Ashkaraz.'

Charlotte Devereaux, all five foot nothing of her, blinked her large silver-blue eyes. Shock was written across her pretty, pink features.

She should be shocked.

She should be quaking in those little boots of hers.

He'd only just been notified of her escape and her jaunt down Kharan's main street, and to say that he was angry was massively to understate the case.

He was furious. Absolutely, volcanically furious.

The fury boiled away inside him like lava, and only long years of iron control kept it locked down and not spilling everywhere, destroying everything in its path.

Because he had no one to blame for this incident but himself. He was the one who'd elected to bring her back to Kharan and not to follow Faisal's advice to return her and her father to the dig site from which they'd come.

No, he'd decided to handle her himself, to make sure she was taken back to Kharan and had the medical treatment she required. Her father had needed more, and was still unconscious in a secure hospital ward. She had been transferred to the facility where they kept all illegal visitors to Ashkaraz.

Normally those visitors tended to be men. They were not usually little women who could wriggle through small windows. He hadn't even known the cell she'd been put in *had* a window.

Not that it mattered now. What mattered was that this woman had escaped and had somehow stumbled unchecked into Kharan, and she had seen through the lies he and his people told the world.

Far from being a nation stuck in time, mired in

poverty and war, it was prosperous and healthy, its population well-cared-for and happy.

And it was a wealthy nation. A *very* wealthy nation.

A nation that had to hide its wealth from the rest of the world or else be torn apart by those desperate to get their hands on it—as had occurred nearly twenty years earlier.

He couldn't allow that to happen again.

He wouldn't.

Catherine had been at the centre of it twenty years ago and now here was Charlotte Devereaux, another foreign woman causing another diplomatic incident.

This time, though, he would not be a party to it, the way he had been with Catherine. He'd learned his lesson and he'd learned it well, and he would not be giving this woman the benefit of the doubt.

'Oh,' she said faintly. 'Oh. I… I see.'

Her voice had a pleasant husk to it. Somewhere along the line she'd lost her scarf, so her silvery blonde hair hung in a loose ponytail down her back, wisps of it stuck to her forehead. The angry red of the sunburn she'd got out in the desert had faded slightly, leaving her pale skin pink. It made the colour of her eyes stand out, glittering like stars. She wore the same pair of loose blue trousers she'd had on in the desert, though the white shirt had gone, leaving in its place a tight-fitting white tank top.

It did not escape his notice that, though she was small, she had a surprisingly lush figure.

'I am sure that you do not see,' he said, forcing those particular observations to one side. 'Because your little excursion has put me in a very difficult position.'

She gave him a cool look that pricked against something inside him like a thorn, needling him. 'Indeed? How so?'

It was not the response he'd hoped for. In fact, nothing of her behaviour was the response he'd hoped for. She should be afraid. As any woman—or any person, for that matter—who'd woken up to find herself in a jail cell would be. Especially given the rumours she must have heard about Ashkaraz.

She should be terrified for her life, not standing there giving him cool looks as if he was nothing more than a mere functionary and not the king of his own country.

'Miss Devereaux,' he said, his anger still raw. 'You are not at all showing proper deference.'

She blinked those glittering silvery eyes again. 'Oh, I'm not? I'm sorry. I don't know the customs—'

'You would curtsey before your queen, would you not?' He cut her off coldly. 'I am king here. My word is law.'

'Oh,' she repeated, lowering her gaze. 'I didn't mean to offend.' Then she made an awkward curtsey, her hands fluttering at her sides.

He narrowed his gaze at her. Was she making fun of him? He didn't think so, but you could never tell with foreigners.

It didn't improve his temper.

Then again, he shouldn't be taking his temper out on her, full stop. A king should be above such things, as his father had always told him. A ruler needed to be hard, cold. Detached from his emotions.

Except he could feel his anger straining at the leash he'd put on it. He wanted her on her knees, begging his forgiveness.

Are you sure that's the only reason you want her on her knees?

Something shifted inside him—a strange pull.

She was…pretty. And, yes, there was a physical attraction there. Perhaps that accounted for the reason this particular woman tried his temper so badly. Not that an attraction would make the slightest difference. As he'd told Faisal out in the desert, he'd treat her exactly the same way he treated every other intruder.

'It is too late for that,' he said implacably. 'You have offended already. You escaped your cell and found your way into the city.'

She was standing with her small hands clasped, but this time the expression on her face wasn't so much cool as uncertain.

'Yes, well…as I was going to explain, I didn't mean to. I just wasn't sure what you were going to do with me or my father.'

'We would have done what we do with all illegal visitors to Ashkaraz. You would have both been sent back to your home country.' He paused. 'But we cannot do that now.'

Her pale brows drew together. 'Why not?'

'Because you have walked down the main street of Kharan and seen the truth.'

'What? You mean all the nice buildings? The new cars and smartphones and things?' Her mouth, full and prettily pink, curved. 'It's such a beautiful city. How is me seeing that a problem?'

'Because you will tell other people, Miss Devereaux.'

What he had to tell her now wouldn't be welcome, yet she had to understand the gravity of the situation.

'And they will tell others, and so it will go on until the whole world learns the truth. And I cannot let that happen.'

She was still frowning. 'I don't understand…'

'Of course you do not. But you will have plenty of time to work it out.'

Another ripple of uncertainty crossed her face. 'That sounds ominous. What do you mean by that?'

'I mean that we cannot send you back to England. We cannot send either of you back to England. You will have to remain in Ashkaraz.' He paused again, for emphasis. 'Indefinitely.'

CHAPTER THREE

CHARLOTTE'S MOUTH HAD gone bone-dry. 'E-Excuse me?' she stuttered. 'I'm sorry, but I thought you said "indefinitely".'

The man—no, the Sheikh—looked at her with the same unyielding merciless stare he'd been giving her ever since he'd walked in here. As if he was furiously angry and trying to hide it. He was doing a very good job of it, but she recognised his expression. It was the same expression her father had used to have when he was furious with her mother and trying very hard not to show it.

Ever since her parents' relationship had broken down she'd become particularly sensitive to suppressed emotion, because even though the shouting had been bad, her parents' silent fury had been worse. It had filled the whole house, making her feel as if she was being crushed slowly in a vice. She'd had to run away when it got like that—except right now there was no-where to run.

Then again, she wasn't the frightened girl she'd been back then. She'd learned to shield herself from people's inconvenient emotions by being cool and polite. Though that boat had long since sailed in this case.

The Sheikh's relentless golden stare was ines-capable. 'I did,' he said succinctly.

'But you can't mean that.' She swallowed. 'You can't just keep us here for...for ever.'

'My word is law, Miss Devereaux,' he said in that implacable way. 'I can do whatever I please.'

A laugh escaped her, even though she hadn't meant it to, and it sounded shrill in the quiet of the office with the fountain playing outside. 'I'm not going to tell anyone what I saw. I promise I won't. Not that I saw anything anyway—a few buildings, nothing much—'

'Your promises are not sufficient.'

There was no answering amusement in his eyes. None in his face either.

Her chest constricted, and there was a kernel of ice sitting in the pit of her stomach. 'That's ri-diculous. No one will even believe me anyway.'

'Some people will. And they will tell others.

And soon there will be more like you, coming across our borders, wanting to see the truth for themselves. It is attention this country cannot afford.'

Abruptly, he turned away, striding around the side of the desk, moving with the lean grace of a panther.

'No, you cannot leave. You will have to remain here.'

'People will come and find us,' she insisted. 'An eminent professor and his daughter can't just go missing in the desert without someone doing something.'

'Plenty of people go missing in the desert.'

He stood behind his desk, a massive, powerful figure, and the sunlight fell on his glossy black hair. Putting his hands on the desktop, he leaned on them, never breaking eye contact with her.

'They will think you got lost and perished.'

'But not without searching for us,' she argued, because this was insane. Preposterous, even. 'You'll have search parties all along your borders, looking for Dad and me. And everyone has heard all the rumours about Ashkaraz. Don't think people won't be looking your way.'

He said nothing for a long moment and she had

the sense that she'd scored a hit. Good. Because right now that kernel of ice in her gut wasn't going away. It was getting bigger, freezing her.

If you'd only waited in the cell...

Charlotte ignored the thought. Instead she took a surreptitious breath and stared back at the Sheikh, completely forgetting the fact that he was actually a sheikh and maybe that was rude. Then again, he'd threatened to keep her prisoner here indefinitely, and that certainly wasn't polite.

'Are you threatening me, Miss Devereaux?' he enquired at last, his voice silky and dark and full of danger.

Charlotte was suddenly keenly aware of how thin was the ice upon which she was standing. She had no power here. None at all. And yet here she was, arguing with the king himself.

'No, I'm not threatening you. I assure you, I wouldn't dare.'

And yet she had to do something. On the one hand she couldn't afford to anger him—not when he was already angry—but on the other she couldn't allow both herself and her father to be buried in a prison cell for the rest of their lives.

Perhaps she should try and appeal to his humanity?

Before she could think better of it, she moved around the side of the desk and put a tentative hand on his arm. 'Please,' she said, looking up at him, trying not to sound as if she was pleading. 'You don't have to do this. You can just let us go and it'll be fine.'

His gaze dropped to her hand on his arm and then moved back up again, and she was suddenly aware that his skin was very warm beneath her hand, that the feel of his muscles was like iron. And she was aware, too, of his scent—warm and spicy and masculine. He was very large, very powerful, and he was watching her like a predator, intense and focused. His gaze was all gold, like a tiger's, and just as hungry.

Something unfamiliar shifted down low inside her…a kind of heat and a very feminine awareness she hadn't experienced before.

She had never bothered with men. While her friends had been out clubbing and on dating apps she'd preferred staying at home with a book. Because after the front row seat she'd had watching her parents' toxic relationship she'd decided she wanted no part of that. It was easier to retreat between the pages of her book, where there were no arguments, no screaming, no suffocating silences or the kind of seething quiet that presaged a major emotional hurricane—where princes remained fantasies and fantasies ended with a kiss.

She'd never missed having a man in her life. Never wanted one. The only kisses she'd had had been in her imagination, and she'd never met anyone who had made her want to think about more than kisses.

But now, feeling the solidity and strength of the Sheikh's arm beneath her hand, being close to his powerful body, aware of his warmth and rich, spicy scent… She couldn't seem to catch her breath.

'Are you aware,' he murmured, and the soft, silky darkness of his voice was totally at odds with the blazing gold of his eyes, 'that touching the Sheikh without permission means death?'

Oh, dear.

Instinctively she tried to jerk away, but he was too quick, his other hand coming down on hers in a blur of motion, pressing her palm to his forearm.

The heat of his hand against her bare skin was scorching, making her pulse accelerate, and all thought was fragmenting under the pressure of his brilliant gaze.

Was this a distraction?

Was he trying to use his male wiles on her to make her forget what she was saying?

That's ridiculous. He's a sheikh. He can do whatever he likes. And why would he use his wiles on you anyway?

That was a very good point. But, regardless, she couldn't let him get to her. He might very well be the king, but she was a British citizen and she had rights. And surely what he was doing was against the Geneva Convention?

'We're nothing to you,' she said, trying not to sound breathless, hoping to appeal to him in terms he might understand. 'We're insignificant English people. If Dad is unconscious, then he hasn't seen anything, and I don't have a lot of friends so I don't have any people to tell anyway. Your secret is safe with me. And if I accidentally do let something slip, then you…you can come to England and arrest me. Your Majesty,' she added, for good measure.

There was a long and suffocating silence and the pressure of his hand over hers was relentless, burning.

He's not going to let you go.

A small burst of unexpected anger broke through her determined calm. No, he couldn't do this. He couldn't insist she stay here indefinitely, couldn't touch her the way he was doing, and he certainly couldn't keep her prisoner. She wasn't going to allow it.

Determined, Charlotte met his gaze head-on. 'If you let us go now, and without a fuss, I won't tell the media I was held here against my will.'

There was another suffocating silence.

'You,' the Sheikh said softly, 'are either very brave or very stupid, and I cannot tell which it is.'

Charlotte's cheeks burned, but she didn't look away. She was probably being the latter rather than the former, in issuing him such a threat, but what choice did she have?

She didn't want her father to suffer for the mistake she'd made. He'd been awarded custody of her after his bitter divorce from her mother, and she'd never wanted him to regret that, even though she knew he did.

Perhaps if she hadn't run away that last time, forcing her parents to call the police and causing all kinds of fuss, then she wouldn't have felt so bad about it. But she had run away. And the next day her mother had called it quits and her father had ended up with her.

She'd always tried to be good after that. Never running away again, never causing a fuss. Trying to be interested in all the things he was interested in and later, when she was an adult, becoming his assistant and general dogsbody, doing whatever was required.

Including getting him imprisoned for life by a dictator.

Her breath came shorter, faster, though she tried to remain calm.

'Well?' She lifted a brow, trying to sound as if she was merely waiting to hear whether he'd like a cup of tea or not, rather than asking what he was going to do about her threat of a diplomatic incident.

He said nothing, just watched her as he spread his fingers out, his hand completely covering her own. His skin was hot, like a brand, with the same heat that burned in the merciless gold of his eyes.

She had angered him, that was clear, and she should be terrified by that. But for some reason she wasn't. He was standing very close, huge and strong and so very powerful, and yet there was something in the heat of his gaze that made her breath catch.

She didn't know quite what it was, but an instinct she hadn't known she possessed told her that she wasn't without power here. That she had the ability to get under this Sheikh's skin.

It made adrenaline rush in her veins, made her want to push, see how far she could go—which was *not* like her at all. She normally ran from anger, not towards it.

His fingers curled around her hand, holding it for a brief, intense moment. Then he pulled it from his arm and let her go, rising to his full height, towering over her.

She could still feel the heat of his fingers as if they'd been imprinted on her skin, and she wanted to put her hand behind her back or in her pocket to hide it, as if it were visible. But there was no hiding from him.

His eyes gleamed briefly, as if he understood something she didn't, making her blush. But all he said was, 'That, Miss Devereaux, is what is commonly known as a threat. And, as I have told you once already, I do not respond well to threats.'

Charlotte opened her mouth to protest, her

heart hammering in her chest. But he must have done something—pressed some button on his desk—because the doors had opened and the guards were coming in.

He said something to them—a sharp order she didn't understand—and suddenly they were on either side of her, hemming her in.

She swallowed hard. 'So is this how you treat guests in your country? You get your guards to drag them back to the cells?'

'We do not have "guests" in this country, Miss Devereaux, and you will not be going back to a cell.'

His fierce gaze shifted to the guards and he nodded to them once.

And then there was no time to say anything more as she was ushered firmly out of the room.

Tariq paced back and forth in front of the window in his office, coldly furious.

It had been a long time since he was quite *this* angry. Then again, it had been a long time since anyone had issued the kind of threat the little Englishwoman had—all cool and polite and straight to his face.

What made her think that she—a mere nobody—could threaten the king of an entire nation? Looking up at him with her big blue eyes, all beseeching, appealing to him as if he had mercy in his heart instead of cold stone.

And then—then!—to put her hand on his arm as if he was an ordinary man...

You are *an ordinary man. You're just angry that you're responding to her as you did to Catherine.*

That the thought was true didn't make it any more welcome. Because he couldn't deny it. He'd ignored the initial pull of attraction, had dismissed it entirely, and yet as soon as she'd touched him he'd felt his body respond as if it had a will of its own.

The light pressure of her fingers on his arm had caused a sudden rush of awareness of her feminine warmth and her small, lush figure next to his. She'd smelled of something sweet and subtle that reminded him of the flowers in the gardens outside—roses, perhaps. And then those eyes looking up into his had got even bigger, her cheeks even pinker, and he'd known she felt the same pull between them that he did: physical chemistry.

He was an experienced man, and he knew well

enough when he was attracted to a woman, and he was attracted to this one. Strongly so. Which did not help his temper in the slightest, considering he was supposed to be treating her the way he treated all intruders.

Physical desire, however, was something easily dealt with. Her threat to him just now and the challenging look in her blue eyes was not. She had him over a barrel and she knew it.

Because if he kept her and her father the British government would certainly have something to say about it, surely?

Yes, their disappearance could be easily explained by some story of their having got lost and perishing in the desert, but search parties would be sent out. Other governments would know the border of his country wasn't far away from the archaeological site, and those rumours that kept people out would also make people suspicious. Enquiries would be made. Questions would be asked. Ashkaraz would receive attention.

And he did *not* want attention—not from the outside world.

The only reason Ashkaraz remained autonomous and free was because its borders were closed and no one knew anything about it. They didn't know about the massive oil wealth upon which the country sat. Or about how that oil was channelled through various private companies so no one would know where it came from. Or about how that wealth came back into the country and was used to pay for hospitals and schools and other social services.

Ashkaraz was wealthy and prosperous but it came at a price—and that price was isolation from a world that would try and take that wealth from them. Because people were greedy. As he knew to his cost.

Tariq came to a stop in front of his desk, his jaw tight, and had to take a moment to uncurl his fingers, relax the tension in his shoulders, dismiss the anger that burned in his gut. He needed to spend some time in the palace gym—that was what he needed. Some boxing or sword practice with an opponent. Or perhaps he needed to call one of the women he sometimes spent the night with, work out his tension that way.

First, though, he needed to decide exactly what to do about his pretty English captive.

He couldn't risk letting her go, so her father would have to stay too—because he couldn't have the man out and about in the world, demanding his daughter's return.

Yes, she might very well promise not to tell anyone about Ashkaraz, but all it would take was one slip, one accidental confession to the wrong person, and curiosity would start. One person would tell another, and then they would tell a couple more, and on it would go. And then, like a rockslide, it would get bigger and bigger. The border incursions they already had would get worse. Until one day Ashkaraz would no longer remain hidden.

He couldn't risk that. The balance was already fragile; he couldn't allow it to tip.

But keeping them both here would garner unwelcome attention too.

Unless she stays here willingly.

That was a possibility. That way she could contact the British authorities, tell them that she was alive and well and not to look for her, because she had chosen to stay here.

It would be the perfect answer to all his problems but for the tiny fact that she was *not* willing.

So how to make her?

The answer to that was obvious: her father.

He could let Professor Devereaux go—he, after

all, had seen nothing—on the understanding that his daughter would tell the British government that she was alive and well and perfectly happy to stay in Ashkaraz.

The idea solved his little diplomatic problem quite nicely, and he was feeling pleased with himself—until thirty minutes into a meeting with Faisal, when his advisor said, 'You won't like what I'm going to say, Your Majesty, but Almasi wants a decision made about his daughter.'

Tariq, who had been standing with one hip propped against the edge of his desk, his arms folded, was instantly irritated. Almasi was a high-ranking member of his government who'd been angling to have his daughter considered as potential sheikha for the past couple of months. His government in general had been putting pressure on him for a couple of years to marry and secure the succession, but Almasi had been particularly vocal. Mainly because he had an of-age daughter whom he thought would be perfect as Tariq's wife.

Tariq disagreed. Almasi's daughter was a nice woman, but he didn't want anything to do with Almasi himself, or his grasping family. That was the problem with the majority of eligible women in Kharan, and in Ashkaraz in general—they were attached to families who wanted to have a stake in determining the way the wealth of their little nation was distributed. Which would have been fine if it was for the good of the country. But Tariq knew it wouldn't be. It would be for the good of only particular families, and that he wouldn't stand for.

Greed wasn't confined only to outsiders.

Catherine's family had certainly been grasping, so he preferred any woman he might consider marrying not to have such connections.

'I am not going to marry his daughter, no matter what he or the government thinks,' Tariq said, his tone absolute.

Faisal was quiet a moment. Then, 'There is the issue of succession,' he said delicately. 'It must be dealt with, as you know.'

Of course he knew. It was a perennial theme.

'The succession does not have to be dealt with now.'

But the other man's dark gaze was far too perceptive. 'I understand why you have been reluctant, sire. After Catherine, who would not be? But, forgive me, you are not getting any younger. And Ashkaraz needs an heir.'

Something dark coiled tightly in Tariq's gut. He didn't want to think about this now. In fact, he never wanted to think about it. And it didn't help that the old man was right. Ashkaraz *did* need an heir. He just didn't want to be forced into providing one. The fact that it was all to do with Catherine and what had happened between them he knew already, but it didn't make him any less reluctant.

A ruler had to separate himself, keep himself apart, and that had always seemed to him the very antithesis of marriage. But then, a royal marriage didn't require much involvement beyond the getting of an heir. Or at least, that was what his father had told him. And since Tariq's mother had died when Tariq was young, and he'd never had an opportunity to observe a marriage for himself, he had no reason to disbelieve him.

Certainly, though, if he wanted to secure the future of his country an heir would need to be provided whether he liked it or not—or, indeed, whether any of the candidates presented for the begetting of said heir were suitable or not.

And they weren't. None of them were.

'If you want an heir, then you must bring me better candidates for a bride,' he said impatiently.

'There are no more suitable candidates.' Faisal seemed unmoved by his impatience. 'As our borders are closed we have removed ourselves from the world stage, so you cannot get a bride from elsewhere.'

Again, his advisor wasn't wrong. About any of it.

Tariq bared his teeth. 'Then where do you suggest I get a bride from? The moon?'

As soon as he said the last word a memory caught at him...of a lock of hair the colour of starlight showing from underneath a black and white scarf. Hair that had caught on his black robes as he'd lifted her onto his horse.

There is your answer.

It was a preposterous idea. Marry the little Englishwoman he'd found in the desert? An archaeological assistant. A woman who wasn't rich or titled? Who wasn't anyone important in any way? A nobody?

She is perfect.

The thought stuck inside him like a splinter.

Catherine hadn't been a nobody. She'd been a rich American from a wealthy family, beautiful and privileged. She'd certainly thought herself entitled to the love of his father the Sheikh, and when that Sheikh hadn't given her what she wanted she'd set her sights on the Sheikh's teenage son...

She'd been greedy, and his father, fully aware of that greed, had kept the secrets of his country's wealth from her. But Tariq hadn't.

She'd promised to stay with him for ever if only he'd tell her how Ashkaraz had got so rich.

And so he'd told her.

A week hadn't even passed before her family and the companies they'd owned had begun to put pressure on Ashkaraz and its parliament, demanding oil rights for themselves by bribing a few of the right people.

It had nearly ripped his country apart.

But Charlotte Devereaux had only her father, and a mother who'd moved away long ago. There were no brothers or sisters. No elderly relatives. There'd be no one to come after her and try to grasp a piece of Ashkaraz's wealth. And, because she wasn't associated with any of the families here either, there'd be no family members in Ashkaraz trying to get rich.

Yes. She was perfect.

You would like her in your bed too.

The memory of her heat next to him coiled

itself tightly inside him. That would not be… unwelcome. It would be a good outlet for his physical desire and, because she was an outsider, he would never be in danger of wanting more than that. She would remain a constant reminder of his failure with Catherine. A constant reminder of the dangers of emotion.

The government wouldn't be happy, and the old families whose influence he was trying to negate would be even less so. But he wasn't here for their happiness. He wasn't here for divisiveness or self-importance. For one family putting itself above another.

He was here to protect his people, and the government would have to accept his choice of wife whether they liked it or not.

The only issue remaining was how to get her to accept it. Because if she hadn't liked the thought of being *held* here indefinitely, she would like the thought of being *married* to him indefinitely even less.

Then again, he wasn't just anyone.

He was the king.

And he had her father. If he made letting the old man go conditional upon her agreeing to marry him she'd naturally have to accept.

He'd have a suite of rooms set aside for her here in the palace, as befitted her future station, and she'd have access to his considerable wealth and power.

Her life here would be very comfortable indeed.

Certainly better than a shared flat in Clapham.

In fact, the more he thought about it, the better the idea became. Marrying Charlotte Devereaux would solve a great many of his existing problems.

'Not the moon, sire,' Faisal said, oblivious to Tariq's stillness and silence. 'We shall simply have to—'

'No need,' Tariq interrupted, pushing himself away from his desk. 'I have a suitable candidate in mind already.'

Faisal didn't often appear shocked, but he certainly seemed so now. 'I thought you said you had none?'

'One has suddenly occurred to me.' Moving around the side of his desk, Tariq sat down. 'Call a meeting of the council,' he ordered, and then smiled. 'I have an announcement to make.'

CHAPTER FOUR

CHARLOTTE WAS TAKEN to what was quite obviously a library—and, given that it was a very beautiful library, she wasn't quite as scared as she otherwise might have been.

Ornate carved wooden bookshelves lined the walls, stretching from the floor to the ceiling, and there were low couches and divans scattered here and there, strewn with brightly coloured silk cushions. Small tables stood near each couch, the perfect height for cups of tea, and if reading palled there was always the view. Because, like the office she'd been in, the library faced the beautiful walled garden and through the open windows the liquid sound of the fountains played.

It was an extremely pleasant place to sit, even with the two armed guards on either side of the door, though it was an odd choice for a place where the Sheikh might keep a prisoner. Not that she was complaining, since it was a million times better than the jail cell she'd expected to be dragged back to.

She wasn't sure how long she'd been there, but it was enough time for her to have inspected the bookshelves and found quite a few English language books in various genres. She would have been happy to curl up with one on one of the divans.

She'd had enough time to wonder, too, what was going on and what the Sheikh was going to do with her.

She should never have threatened him—that had been a mistake. She couldn't think why she had done so, or even where her bravery had come from. She'd only been conscious that for some reason she affected him, and she'd let that little taste of power go to her head.

And now both she and her father would pay for it.

The fear she'd been ignoring collected inside her once more, and it was still there when hours or minutes later—she wasn't sure which—the guards took her out of the library and down some more of the echoing, beautifully tiled and arched hallways. They passed glittering rooms and ornate alcoves, went down some elegant staircases and past yet more colonnaded gardens and fountains.

The Sheikh's palace was beautiful, and if she hadn't been afraid for her life she would have loved looking around it. But she *was* afraid, and all the beauty around her only made her more so.

She had very much hoped she wouldn't be taken back to that jail cell, and she wasn't. Instead she was shown into a series of interconnected rooms like a hotel suite, with big French doors that opened out into yet another walled garden, though this one was smaller. It had a fountain, too, and delightful beds of roses and fruit trees. The rooms were tiled in subtle, glossy variations of white, giving the walls a lovely textured feel. And there were more beautiful silk rugs on the floors dyed in deep, jewel colours, and low couches to sit on strewn with silken cushions.

Charlotte tried to ask the guards what was going on, why she was there and not in a cell, but either they didn't speak English or they'd been instructed not to speak to her, because they ignored her questions, leaving her alone in the rooms before going out and locking the door behind them.

So, still a prisoner, then, but now her cage was a gilded one.

After they'd gone she explored a little, finding that one of the rooms had a huge bed mounded with pillows standing against one wall, while another contained a beautiful tiled bath and a large shower.

She couldn't understand why the Sheikh was holding her here, in rooms that seemed more appropriate for a visiting head of state than for some illegal alien he'd picked up unconscious in the desert.

None of it made sense.

Left with nothing else to do, Charlotte paced around the main living area of the suite, her brain ticking over. She didn't know why she was here and not in a cell, and she didn't know what was going to happen to her or her father other than that the Sheikh wasn't letting either of them go.

That made her feel cold inside—not for herself, but for her father. He was an eminent professor with a career back in London, and lots of friends and colleagues, and he would hate to be separated from any of it.

Especially when he finds out that all of this is your fault.

The cold inside her deepened.

She'd been the one to break the window and go looking around outside. If she had simply stayed put, then her father would be safe and so would she. Maybe they'd even be on their way back to the border and none the wiser about Ashkaraz.

But that wasn't what had happened.

And if it's your fault, then it's up to you to fix it.

That was true. But how?

She came to a stop in front of the windows, looking at the pretty rose garden outside, thinking.

There really was only one way to fix it. She was the one who'd blundered out onto the street and seen what she shouldn't have, not her father. He was blameless. Maybe she could convince the Sheikh to let him go if she agreed to remain here? She didn't have a career, like her father did, or friends. No one would miss her.

Your father wouldn't miss you either.

Charlotte pushed that thought aside, hurrying on with her idea. The professor surely wouldn't argue with her, and she could reassure him that everything was fine so he wouldn't think she was being held against her will. She could reassure the British authorities too—keep them away from Ashkaraz's borders, appease the Sheikh.

An unexpected shiver went through her as she thought of him again. Of his intensely masculine, powerful physical presence. His large hand over hers, his palm burning against her skin. The hard muscles of his forearm and his fierce golden stare. The anger she had sensed burning inside him no matter how cold his expression.

Could she appease a man like him? Did she have the power? But she'd got to him in some way earlier, she knew it, so maybe she could do it again.

If she wanted to save her father she would have to.

And what about you? Staying in a strange country all alone for the rest of your life?

Charlotte ignored that. She'd deal with it later. Right now, making sure her father was safe was more important.

The time ticked past and she spent it exploring the small suite of rooms and admiring them in between wondering what on earth was going on and trying to keep her feelings of panic at bay.

At last the doors opened, admitting two exquisitely robed women. One carried a tray of food, the other an armful of silvery blue fabric. The woman with the tray put it down on a small table near the window, while the other laid the fabric across a low divan nearby.

'Tonight you will dine with His Majesty, Sheikh Tariq Ishak Al Naziri,' said the woman near the tray in lightly accented English. She gestured at the fabric spread out on the divan. 'His Majesty has provided suitable attire for you and some refreshment in the meantime. I will come and collect you at the designated hour.'

Charlotte stared at the woman in astonishment. Attire? Refreshment? *Dining?*

What on earth was going on?

'But why?' she burst out. 'And what about my father? Why am I being kept here? What does the Sheikh want with me?'

But the woman only smiled and shook her head, and then she and the other woman turned around and went out, leaving Charlotte alone again.

Okay, so clearly no one was going to answer her questions. Which meant she would have to get answers from His Majesty Sheikh Tariq himself. And she was not going to be put off again by his golden stare and his gentlemanly wiles.

She would insist he answered her and then she'd request that he send her father home.

The thought made her feel a little better, so she helped herself from the small tray of food—flat-bread still warm from the oven and spicy dips, along with some fresh fruit. Once she'd eaten, she wandered into the bathroom to examine it in greater detail—and then decided that if the Sheikh was housing her in such luxurious accommodation she was going to take advantage of that fully.

So she stripped off her dirty clothing and had a long, hot shower, using delicious rose-scented body wash and shampoo. After her shower, wrapped in a big fluffy white towel, she went back into the living area where the 'suitable attire' had been spread over the divan near the window.

The 'attire' proved to be very pretty robes in silvery blue silk, with roses embroidered around the edge in heavy silver thread. Charlotte put out a hand and gently touched the fabric. It was cool and soft beneath her fingertips. But he'd provided this for her, and part of her didn't want to wear it purely because he'd told her to. Part of her wanted to turn up to this dinner in her own filthy clothes and to hell with him.

But she didn't allow herself such petty rebellions these days—plus, there was no point in angering him needlessly. Not when she had her father's safety to consider as well as her own. Also, she didn't know his country's customs, and causing offence purely because she was angry would be stupid.

Better to wear the robes…be polite, courteous. And then tell him what was what.

Besides… She stroked the fabric again, enjoying the feel of it. The robes were beautiful and she'd never worn anything like them before. Princesses in fairy tales always wore beautiful dresses, and as a child she'd often wished she could have a beautiful dress too. But her mother had never been particularly interested in what Charlotte had wanted. She'd never been interested in Charlotte at all.

You're a prisoner in a strange country, with no idea of what the future will hold for you, and yet you're thinking about how nice it will be to wear a pretty dress?

Well, why not? Her own clothes were filthy, and who knew what was going to happen to her afterwards? She might never get the opportunity to wear a pretty dress ever again.

Dropping the towel, Charlotte dressed herself in the robes, feeling the fabric deliciously cool and smooth against her skin. Then she went to stand in front of the full-length mirror in the bedroom and adjusted the material. She looked… nice, she had to admit. And she felt a little more in control now she was clean and dressed—even in 'suitable attire'.

If she was going to beg a favour from a king, she'd better look the part.

The robed women didn't come back for a long while, and Charlotte tried to fill in the time by examining every inch of her suite and then by having a small nap.

At last the light began to fade, and then a knock came at the door. It opened to reveal one of the robed women.

Charlotte pushed herself up from the divan she'd been sitting on, her heart thumping hard in her chest. The woman gave her a brief survey and there was a satisfied look in her eyes that made Charlotte feel a tiny bit better. Obviously her choice to wear the robes had been a good one.

'His Majesty will see you now,' the woman said. 'Please follow me.'

Nervously clasping her hands in front of her, Charlotte did so, noting the two guards that fell into step behind her as she left the suite.

The corridors were silent but for the sound of the guards' boots on the tiled floor. Her own steps were muffled by the pair of silver slippers she'd put on, which had come with the robes.

She tried to take note of where they were going, but after a few twists and turns, more stairs and more long corridors, she gave up, looking at the high arched ceilings instead, and the glittering tiles on them that caused the light to refract and bounce. They were beautiful, and she got so lost in them that for a couple of minutes at least she forgot that she was going to meet the terrifying man who was king.

Eventually the hallway opened up, and to her delight Charlotte found herself stepping out into the colonnaded garden she'd seen through the windows of the Sheikh's office. The air was as cool and soft as the silk she wore, and laden with the scent of flowers and the gentle sound of the fountains splashing.

The woman led her along a path to the central fountain itself, and then stopped and gestured.

Charlotte's breath caught.

In the dim twilight, tea lights in exquisite glass holders leapt and danced. They'd been set on a low table, their flames illuminating the multitude of cushions set on the ground around it and glittering off glasses and cutlery. Bowls full of food sat on the table—sliced meats and dips and more of the flatbread.

It was like something straight out of one of her favourite books, *The Arabian Nights*, and for a second she could only stand there and stare.

Then she became aware of the man sprawled on one of the cushions at the table, watching her. He rose as she approached, fluidly and with grace, until he towered over the table and her, the candle flames making his golden eyes glow.

He wasn't wearing the suit trousers and shirt she'd seen him in earlier that day but black robes, their edges heavily embroidered in gold thread. They suited him, highlighting his height and the broad width of his shoulders, and the sense of power that rolled off him in waves.

The flickering light illuminated his face, and his features were set in a fierce sort of expression that made her heart race. He wasn't angry now, it seemed, but he'd definitely decided something—though what it could be she had no idea.

What jailer set out a beautiful dinner like this if a prison cell was all that awaited her? It didn't make any sense.

'Welcome, Miss Devereaux.'

His deep voice prowled over her skin, soft and dark as a panther.

'Thank you for joining me.'

Charlotte resisted the urge to shift on her feet, uncomfortable as his intense gaze roved over her. She didn't know how she knew, but she had the sense that he liked what he saw. Which made it difficult to think.

'Well,' she said stoutly, pulling herself together. 'It wasn't like I had a choice.'

The corner of his hard mouth curved and for a second Charlotte couldn't do anything but stare at him, her breath catching at the beauty of his smile.

'That is true,' he acknowledged. 'But I am glad you came without the necessity of guards dragging you.'

It was very clear that if she had refused then, yes, the guards would have dragged her to meet him.

Fear flickered through her, and the old urge to run away and hide gripped her. But she ignored it, steeling herself. Best to get this out of the way first.

'Your Majesty,' she began formally. 'I've been thinking and I want to—'

'Please,' the Sheikh interrupted, gesturing to the table. 'Sit.'

'No, thank you.' Charlotte's palms were sweaty, her heart showing no sign of slowing down. She needed to say this and fast—before she changed her mind. 'I know that you've decided not to let my father and me leave, but I have a request to make.'

His expression was impassive. 'Do you, indeed?'

'Yes, I think—'

'Sit, Miss Devereaux. We shall have this discussion as we eat.'

'No. I need to say this now.' She took an unsteady breath, meeting his fierce golden stare. 'If you let my father go, I'll stay here. And I'll do so willingly.'

* * *

Tariq said nothing, watching Charlotte Devereaux's pale face in the flickering candlelight. It was obvious she'd been thinking hard in the time she'd been cooling her heels in the sheikha's suite. And he had to admire her courage; it couldn't be easy, facing a lifetime in a strange land, even if it meant her father went free.

But that was good. She would need that courage and she would need strength too, for the role he would give her. The sheikha would need both.

She certainly made a pretty picture, standing there in the robes he'd chosen for her. The silver-blue suited her pale skin and deepened the colour of her eyes. She'd clearly washed her hair, and it lay soft and loose over her shoulders and down her back, the pale mass curling slightly.

He was pleased she'd worn the robes, and pleased that she'd decided to make an effort. Because that was all part of his plan.

The council had been in an uproar at his abrupt choice of wife, as he'd expected, so he'd deliberately had the robes sent to her, and then had her walked through the palace so everyone could observe the picture of quiet elegance and strength that she presented.

He hadn't been certain she would wear the robes, or that she wouldn't make a fuss about attending his dinner, but he'd counted on her English manners preventing her from making a scene and so far he'd been proved right.

He was pleased with that too.

And now she'd just volunteered to stay willingly if he let her father go, which made things even easier.

Don't feel too pleased with yourself. You haven't told her about the marriage yet.

No, he hadn't. He'd hoped to take his time with his proposal, feeding her the excellent food his chefs had provided and pouring her wine from his extensive cellars. And then perhaps some civilised conversation to set her at ease.

But, judging from the fear in her pretty blue eyes and the way she had her hands clasped together, spinning it out might not be such a good idea. Her finely featured face was set in lines of determination and she was standing very straight, as if bracing herself for a blow, so maybe he should deliver it. A quick, clean strike.

The candlelight glittered off the silver in her

robes and glimmered in her lovely hair, making her look like a fall of moonlight in the darkness of the garden. And it prompted something to shift uncomfortably inside his chest—something that felt a lot like sympathy.

Which was wrong. He couldn't afford to be sympathetic. He had been sympathetic with Catherine the night he'd found her weeping beside this very fountain, and his heart—the traitor—had twisted inside his chest at the sight of her tears.

Sympathy was not the only thing you felt that night, remember?

Of course he remembered. How could he forget? He'd also been angry, burning with a frustrated rage that he hadn't been able to control. A volatile cocktail of emotion that had turned dangerous in the end.

He wouldn't do that again.

He had to be hard, cold. Ruthless. He couldn't risk being anything else.

'That is certainly a brave request,' he said, ignoring the tightness in his chest. 'You might change your mind when you hear mine.'

She blinked in surprise. 'Y-Yours?'

Tariq dropped his gaze to the cushions opposite. 'Sit down, Miss Devereaux.'

He didn't make it sound like anything less than the command it was, and after a brief hesitation she took a couple of faltering steps towards the table, then sat down awkwardly on the cushions.

Satisfied, he sat down himself, studying her pale face. And, even though he thought he'd shoved aside that brief burst of sympathy he'd experienced, he found himself pouring her a glass of the cool white wine and then putting a few tasty items of food on a plate for her.

It was the custom in Ashkaraz for a prospective groom to woo his potential wife by feeding her, so the dinner had been organised very deliberately, to make sure everyone knew exactly what his intentions were. But right now all he was conscious of was that she was quite pale, and that possibly the food he'd had sent to her room hadn't been enough. She really needed to have something more substantial—especially given what he was going to tell her.

He pushed the wine glass in her direction, and then the plate of food. 'You should eat.'

Her pretty mouth tightened, full and lush and pink. 'No, thank you. I'm not hungry.'

Her chin had lifted and there was a slight but unmistakable glow of defiance in her blue eyes.

Faintly amused by her show of spirit, despite himself, he nearly smiled. 'If you want to spite me, there are other, better ways of doing so.'

Colour tinged her cheeks. 'Oh, yes? And what are those?'

'Any number of things—but if you think I am going to tell you what they are, you are mistaken.'

She narrowed her gaze, ignoring the food and the wine. 'Excuse me, Your Majesty, but what is all this for? This dinner? The rooms I was locked in? These…clothes?'

One small hand went to the embroidered edge of her robe, the tips of her fingers running over it. She liked it, he could tell, even though she probably didn't want to.

'I thought I was your prisoner.'

'If you were truly my prisoner you would be back in that jail cell.'

'But you said I was to be here indefinitely. That I was—'

'That is part of the request I have to make,' he interrupted calmly. 'Though perhaps you should have a sip of wine and something to eat before we discuss it.'

Little sparks glittered in her eyes. 'Like I said, I'm not hungry.'

Well, if she didn't want to eat he certainly wasn't going to force her, and nor should he draw this out any longer than he had to.

What happened to a quick, clean strike?

She and her white face had happened.

She and the sympathy that seemed to sit in the centre of his chest whether he wanted it to or not.

'Do not eat, then.' He shoved that sympathy aside once again. 'It makes no difference to what I have to say to you.'

Her gaze narrowed even further, but she didn't speak, merely sat on the cushions, as straight-backed and dignified as the sheikha she would soon be.

'The safety of my country is of paramount importance to me, Miss Devereaux,' he began, holding her gaze so he could see that she under-stood. 'And protecting it is my purpose as king—a purpose I take very seriously indeed. So when the safety of my country is compromised I must take certain steps.'

'I see. Such as keeping me here, despite the fact that I'm not a threat?'

She was still angry, and he supposed he couldn't blame her. Not when she didn't know the history of the country she was dealing with.

Or your role in it.

But she didn't need to know that. No one did. It was enough that he was working to fix the mistake he'd made, and fix it he would.

'It is not you who gets to decide what is a threat to Ashkaraz and what is not.' He didn't bother to hide the chill in his voice. 'That is my decision.'

Again, colour crept through her cheeks, but she didn't look away. 'You were talking about certain steps. What are they?'

'Keeping you here is definitely one of them. But there are other threats to my kingdom that have nothing to do with you.'

'Okay—fine. I get that. But I still don't understand what this has to do with giving me dinner.'

'A kingdom can be threatened from within as well as without. And there are certain families who put themselves first, over the people of this country.'

He could feel the anger gathering in him again. Cold and terrible anger at the web of alliances that had been forged purely for personal gain and how those very same people who had taken advantage of his father's generosity now looked to take advantage of his.

'I will not have it,' he went on, his voice on the edge of a growl. 'I will not have my council or my government divided, and I will not have one family being awarded more importance than another.'

Her defiance had melted away, and he saw a bright curiosity burning in her eyes. 'No. I can imagine not. But I'm not sure what this has to do with me.'

He bared his teeth. 'If you let me finish, I will tell you.'

She gave a little sniff. 'I wasn't interrupting. Please, go on.'

Her hand moved to the wine glass and she picked it up, taking a sip. Then she looked down at the plate he'd set in front of her and idly picked up an olive, popping it into her mouth.

Clearly she was hungrier than she'd said. Satisfaction moved through him that she was finally eating the food he'd presented to her, allaying his anger somewhat.

'I need a wife, Miss Devereaux,' he said,

watching her. 'The royal succession must be ensured and my council wish this to happen soon. But I will not give in to factions—which means I cannot choose a bride from within my own country. There is no shortage of candidates, but none are suitable.'

Her brow wrinkled as she put the olive pit on her plate, then picked up another olive, chewing thoughtfully. 'That's unfortunate. Can't you choose a bride from outside the country?'

'Our borders are closed—so, no, I cannot.'

'That's *very* unfortunate, in that case.' Once she'd finished the olive she picked up some flatbread, dipping it in the hummus he'd spread on her plate. 'Isn't there anyone you can choose?'

'Not from among the candidates that have been put before me. They all have families who are greedy, grasping. Who want political influence.'

'You can't just tell them no?'

There was no anger at all in her expression now. Her attention was focused on the puzzle of finding him a wife. And if she found it strange that he was discussing it with her, she didn't show it.

Why are you explaining yourself to her? You

are the king. Your word is law. Simply tell her she will be marrying you and be done with it.

The thought needled at him. Because explaining was exactly what he was doing and he wasn't sure why.

Perhaps it had something to do with her initial fear and then that little spark of defiance. And the way she'd absently started eating, no matter that she'd made a point of telling him she wasn't hungry.

There was something artless and innocent to her that he found attractive, and it was very much the opposite of what he was used to from the people around him. They were all greedy, all wanted something from him, and they were never honest about it. They lied and manipulated, as Catherine had done, to get what they wanted.

No wonder his father had taught him that isolation was the best lesson for any ruler. To rely on his own judgement and not be swayed by anyone or anything, still less the promptings of his own heart.

Once he'd thought his father had been wrong—but that had been before Catherine, before he'd learned otherwise, and now he filled his heart with marble and his will with steel. Nothing got through. Nothing made him bend.

How does that explain the sympathy in your heart for this woman?

He didn't know. And he didn't like it.

'I cannot "tell them no",' he said flatly. 'Not outright. That would cause more division and dissension, so I must be cautious.'

She frowned. 'Then how are you supposed to find a wife?'

Did she really have no idea what he was leading up to? Did she really not understand?

Tariq searched her face, seeing only puzzlement. 'I have found one.'

Only then did something flicker in her eyes— a flash of apprehension. 'Oh?'

He stared at her, looking for what he didn't know. 'You are not going to ask me who it is?'

Her mouth opened and then closed, and then she tore her gaze from his, looking down at her plate. Her hands dropped to her lap. The candle-light glittered off her pale lashes and her hair, giving her an ethereal, fragile air.

And that strange feeling in his chest, that sympathy that wouldn't go away, deepened. He fought it, because it couldn't gain ground in him.

He wouldn't let anything like it take root inside him again.

There was silence and he waited.

Because she'd guessed—he was sure of it—and he wanted her to say it.

'You can't...' she murmured, not looking up. 'You can't mean...me.'

'Can I not?'

Her lashes quivered against the smooth, pale skin of her cheeks and she went very still, tension radiating from her. 'I don't understand,' she said eventually.

'What is there to understand? I need a wife, Miss Devereaux. I need the succession secured and I need my council happy. And I need to put those aristocratic families seeking to use their position to their advantage back in their place.' He paused, making sure that soft, weak feeling inside him was gone. 'I had no suitable candidates, no prospect of any, and then you turned up. You are perfect for the role.'

There was more silence, broken only by the splashing of the fountain. She didn't move, kept her gaze on the table, but he could almost feel her shock.

'You have no family except your father,' he

went on. 'And, more importantly, you have no family here. Which means there will be no one using you to better themselves or their position. You are an outsider with no connections, and that makes you ideal.'

Her long, pale throat moved. 'But…but I'm just a woman you picked up in the desert. A nobody.'

'Which is precisely why you are perfect.'

She looked up suddenly and he thought he saw a flicker of hurt in her eyes. But then it was gone and the anger was back.

'You can't marry me,' she said. 'I'm sorry, but you just can't.'

'Give me one good reason.'

'I don't even know you, for God's sake.' Her face had become quite pink. 'We only just met this morning.'

He shouldn't, but he couldn't deny that he liked her sudden display of temper. He preferred a woman with spirit, and outrage was better than fear.

'Knowing someone is not any prerequisite for a royal marriage that I am aware of,' he said calmly. It would no doubt aggravate her, but she could do with a little more aggravation. It would give her something to fight against. 'And we will have plenty of time to get to know one another.'

'You're assuming I'm going to go through with it,' she shot back. 'Well, just a heads-up for you: I'm not. And you can't make me.'

He wished he didn't have to. But he was going to.

'*Au contraire*, Miss Devereaux. I can certainly make you. For example, if you do not agree, then your father will remain here as my guest. Along with yourself.'

The pink in her cheeks deepened, creeping down her neck. 'So you're going to use Dad to force me to marry you? Is that what you're saying?'

For a second he allowed himself a shred of regret that he had to do this to her, that he couldn't simply let her go back to her life in England along with her father.

Then he excised that regret from his soul. He couldn't let her return to her life. He had a duty to his country to fix the mistake he'd made all those years ago, when he'd put his own feelings ahead of what was best for his nation.

It was a mistake he would not make again.

'Yes,' he said, making his voice hard. 'That is exactly what I am saying.'

Temper glittered in her eyes, stronger this time. 'What about me? What about my wishes? What if I don't want to marry you?'

He met her furious blue gaze. 'I am afraid that you do not get a say. If you do not agree, I will keep your father here.'

She took a little breath, her jaw tight. 'Then maybe he'll have to stay here. He might even like it. It might be just the kind of thing he'd enjoy.'

It was a bluff and they both knew it.

'Are you saying that your father would enjoy being cut off from his colleagues?' Tariq asked. 'From his position as professor? He is an eminent man. He is used to having respect—used to having intellectual discourse with his peers. How will he cope being cut off from all of that? And what will he think of your choice? Because as much as I am choosing for you, you are choosing for him.'

That lovely lush mouth of hers tightened again, and the glow of anger in her eyes was even more intense. She wasn't so much a fall of moonlight now but an angry storm, full of lightning and thunder. A passionate woman.

You will enjoy exploring just how passionate.

Oh, yes, he would. Very much so.

Oblivious to the tenor of his thoughts, she said angrily, 'You have an answer for everything, don't you?'

'Of course. I am the king.' He softened his voice to mollify her. 'It will not be so bad, *ya amar.* As my wife, you will be sheikha. You will have access to my wealth and power. You may live whatever life you choose as long as it does not threaten this country or its people.'

She remained determinedly unmollified. 'Essentially, though, I will still be your prisoner.'

'You will be my prisoner whether you marry me or not.'

His patience was beginning to fray now, because people generally did whatever he wanted them to do, and if he told them to jump they asked *How high?* They did not sit there arguing with every word he said.

'The only thing you have to do, Miss Devereaux, is determine your choice of cage.'

CHAPTER FIVE

CHARLOTTE SAT ACROSS from the Sheikh, conscious of only one prevailing emotion: anger.

She simply could not believe what he'd said.

Marry him? Marry the *king*?

Her heart was fluttering like a furious bird in her chest, her pulse wild beneath her skin, and she had a horrible feeling it wasn't only anger that she was feeling. But, since anger was preferable to anything else, she clung on tightly to it.

He'd explained why he'd chosen her and yet it still didn't make any sense.

Yes, she was a nobody, with no connections—a foreigner, an outsider. But did he really need to keep emphasising how alone and common she was? Or was that in order to make her feel isolated? So that she felt she wouldn't have any choice but to marry him?

Not that his motives were the most important thing right now.

Not when all she could think about was the word 'marriage'.

It made her feel cold all over. Because all she could think about was her parents, screaming at each other. And when they hadn't been screaming, there had been dreadful silences full of resentment and bitterness.

Not all marriages were like that, she knew, but her parents' marriage had put her off for life, and nothing she'd seen so far had made her want to change her mind—still less the thought of being married to this...complete stranger.

She didn't want to marry him.

She didn't want to marry anyone.

You might not have a choice.

It certainly seemed that way, since it was obvious he felt very strongly about protecting his country. In fact, the way he'd spoken about his purpose had fascinated her, and she'd been intrigued by the conviction glowing in his eyes.

Until he'd spoiled it by telling her that she was going to be his wife.

He was staring at her now, apparently impervious to the anger rising inside her. The planes and angles of his face were impassive, his golden stare cold. He looked like a god of ancient times, weighing the contents of her soul, determining whether she would go to heaven or hell.

Except that it was she who had to make the decision. Or at least he'd given her the illusion that she did. And illusion it was, since either she married him or he kept her father in Ashkaraz.

How is this any different from you staying here in return for your father's freedom?

It was *very* different. Before, she'd imagined she'd simply be allowed to have a life here—and, though she hadn't thought about that life in any detail, it hadn't seemed as depressingly final as marriage.

She had a brief vision of herself doing something completely and uncharacteristically violent, such as hurling the contents of her wine glass in his face or upending the table, but that felt far too close to something her mother or her father might have done, so she ignored it.

Instead, she forced herself to sit very still, her jaw tight, her back rigid. 'And if I decide to be a prisoner and not marry you?'

The food she'd eaten sat uncomfortably in her stomach. His straight dark brows drew together and the effect made her breath catch. He was forbidding in his black robes and that slight frown only made him more so.

'Then you are quite welcome to return to the cell you escaped from.' His voice was as dark and deep as the ocean. 'And your father with you.'

A quiver went through her. Return to that small, cramped, bare room? With the bucket in the corner? And the hard bed? And her father too… He would hate it and she knew he would. The horrible Sheikh was right. He would hate being cut off from his colleagues, from his work, from his life back in England.

Another thing to blame you for.

Charlotte swallowed. She'd tried so hard to be good for him, but sometimes she wondered if it would ever be enough. Perhaps this sacrifice finally would be? After all, it *was* her mistake that had got them into this mess.

You're seriously contemplating marriage to this man?

Maybe. Maybe it wouldn't be as bad as she thought. Her parents had once thought themselves in love, and that was why it had gone so wrong—or at least that was what her father had told her. Love turned toxic, was a recipe for disaster.

This would be a different kind of marriage from the one her parents had had right from the start, since she barely knew this man, let alone loved him. There would be no toxic emotion since she had no emotion about him to begin with.

That's a lie.

Charlotte chose to ignore that particular thought.

Her hand shook as she reached for her wine glass, taking a sip of the cool liquid. It was pleasantly dry, as she preferred her wine to be, and soothed her aching throat.

The Sheikh merely watched her with those predatory tiger's eyes.

'Why are you bothering with this?' she snapped in sudden temper, uncomfortable and not knowing what to do with herself. 'The dinner? The robes? Why are you even bothering to ask me? When you could simply drag me down the aisle and make me say "I do" right now?'

'Because I am not a monster—even though I might appear to be one. And I thought you would appreciate at least the illusion of choice.'

'Yes, well…' She put the glass down with a click, splashing the wine slightly. 'I don't appreciate it.'

He tilted his head, watching her. 'You are angry.'

'Of course I'm bloody—'

'Angry rather than scared. Why is that?'

She didn't want to answer. Because she had a horrible feeling that she was, in fact, scared, and that if she thought too much about it she'd end up scurrying away like a frightened mouse. And she couldn't do that. Not in front of a predator like him.

Instead, she clutched her courage and lifted her chin higher. 'There's not much point in being scared, is there? That's not going to get me very far.'

'Anger will not either,' he pointed out. 'Though anger is a far more useful emotion.'

'It's not very useful right now. Especially since I'm assuming that emptying my wine glass in your face will result in my death?'

Unexpectedly a flicker of something crossed his features. It was gone too fast for her to tell what it was, but she caught the gleam of it in his eyes, fierce and hot and completely at odds with the cold expression that had been there before.

It was almost as if he liked her anger, even approved of it, which was a strange thing to think. Yet she couldn't shake the thought, and for reasons she couldn't have explained knowing that somehow eased her fear and bolstered her courage.

'I would not recommend doing it.'

A thread of something she didn't recognise wound through this dark voice.

'So, I take it you accept my proposal?'

She glared at him. 'Do you need my acceptance?'

'No.' There was no sympathy in the word, and yet no triumph either. It was simply a statement of fact.

'So why the need for all…' she waved a hand to encompass the table and the robes she wore '…all of this?'

The fierce glow in his eyes was still there, and the way he sat back on the cushions, large and muscular and dangerous, sent an inexplicable thrill arrowing down her spine.

This man was going to be her husband.

And you know what that means, don't you?

It should have occurred to her before, and yet it hadn't—the realisation that marriage didn't just mean standing up and vowing to love one another till death do you part. There was another part of a relationship that marriage brought, wasn't there? A part she'd had no experience with whatsoever.

Sex.

An unfamiliar feeling twisted, right down deep inside her, and though fear was a part of it, it wasn't the only part. There was something else too—something to do with that thrill at the warmth of his body she'd experienced earlier that day and the feel of his arm beneath her hand. The awareness of him, of the amount of space he took up, an entirely physical awareness…

Her mouth went dry and she wanted to look away, suddenly sure that he could see exactly what she was thinking, exactly what realisation she was only just now coming to. Because those golden eyes would see everything.

She reached for the wine again, picking it up and taking another desperate sip to moisten her throat, her heartbeat thudding in her ears.

He couldn't want her to have sex with him, surely? She wasn't beautiful. She wasn't experienced. He would have his pick of lovely women as king, and he definitely wouldn't ever have picked her—not if she hadn't turned up so conveniently out in the desert.

He's mentioned securing the succession.

Yes, he had, but still...

'You have a question?'

His voice wrapped around her, velvety and soft in the darkness, as if he knew exactly what she was thinking.

'Ask me.'

She should, she knew that, but she couldn't bear the thought. She didn't know what she would do if he told her that, no, sex with him would not be required. Or what she would do if he said that, yes, it would.

Probably burst into flames with embarrassment either way.

'N-No,' she stuttered. 'I don't have a question.'

She steeled herself to meet his gaze. And she didn't understand the glitter in his eyes, because it looked like anger, and yet she didn't think it was. It was far too intent, far too focused.

'Open your mouth, *ya amar*,' he ordered quietly.

It was not what she'd expected him to say and

it took her by surprise—so much so that she'd already opened her mouth to obey him before she realised what she'd done.

Snapping it shut almost immediately, she gave him a suspicious look. 'Why?'

He leaned forward and picked up one of the strawberries sitting in a silver bowl. 'It is the custom in Ashkaraz for a prospective groom to feed his chosen bride. So open your mouth, Miss Devereaux, and signify your acceptance.'

This time there was no doubt about the sharp-edged glitter in his eyes. It was all challenge. And even though she didn't want to obey him, she felt something rise up inside her in response.

It was just a stupid strawberry. And maybe it was a custom here, but it didn't mean anything to her.

It means you accept that you will marry him.

Well, she had no choice about that. And if she had to stay here indefinitely surely it would be better to stay here as the sheikha—whatever that meant—than it would be as a prisoner in a cell.

And who knew? If she was queen maybe she could even change things for herself. Influence him to open up the borders so she could go home eventually. It was an idea. She didn't have to simply bow to his wishes for ever.

The decision hardened inside her and she caught his gaze with hers, letting him know that she wasn't going to lie down and be his doormat no matter what he thought. Then she leaned forward slightly and opened her mouth.

A flame leapt in his eyes, and though she didn't know what it meant, something deep inside her did, and it was making her heartbeat race, all her awareness focus abruptly on him.

He held out the strawberry, brushing the fruit along her mouth at first, tracing her lower lip in an almost-caress that made her mouth feel full and oddly sensitive, made another little shiver snake down her spine.

She went still as he did it again, this time tracing her upper lip with the strawberry before placing it gently in her mouth and holding onto the stem.

'Bite down, *ya amar*,' he ordered, and she did, sweetness bursting onto her tongue. Then he withdrew his hand, taking the stem with it, his fingers brushing her lower lip and leaving a trail of hot sparks in its wake.

Charlotte swallowed the strawberry, but she

wasn't concentrating on the taste. All she could feel was the brush of his fingers on her mouth, and she nearly raised a hand and touched her lips herself.

He was watching her, and she didn't know what he'd seen in her face but something had satisfied him, she was sure. That hot, golden glow was burning in his eyes again and she still didn't know what it meant.

You do. Come on.

Maybe. But she didn't want to think about that. Didn't want to think about why her mouth felt so sensitive and why her heart was beating so hard. Why there was an unfamiliar ache down low inside her.

'Well?' she said thickly, trying to pretend that ache wasn't there. 'Is that all I need to do, then?'

He dropped the stem back in the bowl 'That is all.'

'Good.'

Her hands were shaking and she didn't like it. Suddenly all she wanted was to be alone, away from here. Away from *him*.

'I—I'm tired, Your Majesty. If you don't mind, I'd like to go back to...' She gestured at the doorway into the palace, then pulled at her robes, getting awkwardly to her feet without waiting for his agreement.

He rose far more fluidly than she and her heartbeat became a roar as he moved around the table towards her, all tall, dark muscularity, the hem of his robes flaring out around his booted feet.

'Oh, no…it's okay.'

She took an unconscious step back, as if putting some physical distance between herself and him would separate her from the strange feeling careering around in her chest. A feeling that she suspected might be excitement even though it also felt like fear. A feeling she didn't want, whatever it was.

'I can find my way back myself.'

The Sheikh stopped, candlelight flickering off the gold embroidery of his robes, and she thought she caught amusement in his eyes. But then it was gone.

'Very well.' He raised a hand and instantly the robed woman stepped out of the shadows of the doorway, as if she'd been standing there waiting for his command all this time. 'Amirah, please escort Miss Devereaux back to her suite.' In the darkness his eyes gleamed, a tiger on the prowl. 'Sleep well, *ya amar*. Tomorrow you will be busy.'

Heartbeat thumping, Charlotte let herself be led away.

'Excuse me, Amirah,' she said hesitantly as they went down the echoing, dimly lit corridors. 'What does *ya amar* mean?' It had been bothering her.

'It means "my moon",' Amirah murmured. 'Or "my most beautiful". It is an endearment.'

Charlotte felt her cheeks get hot. His "most beautiful"? Well, that was a lie. She wasn't beautiful and she certainly wasn't his.

But soon you will be.

Charlotte ignored the shiver that went down her spine at the thought.

It wasn't excitement. It just wasn't.

She didn't see the Sheikh over the next couple of days, which was a good thing. And she might have spent those days pacing around in her suite, reflecting over and over on the wisdom of her decision, had not Amirah turned up at her door the next day, informing her that she was now to be Charlotte's assistant and had been asked to help her with the list of tasks His Majesty had assigned to her. Then she'd brandished said list and Charlotte, craving distraction, had grabbed it with some relief.

The Sheikh had asked her to familiarise herself with the history, customs, people and language of Ashkaraz, which made sense since she was going to be queen. And since she'd always found learning interesting she'd thrown herself into study with abandon, especially as it involved spending a lot of time in the beautiful library she'd been taken to when she'd first got to the palace.

There were also culture and protocol lessons—which she found very interesting too—not to mention a lot of scrubbing and oiling of her body—which she found less interesting—including plucking and face masks and hair wraps. The beautification process for an Ashkarazi bride, apparently.

In between all of this the Sheikh sent updates on her father's condition and then, on the third day, a note to say that the professor had been taken to the border and would be released within hours. She was to send him an email, confirming her decision to stay in Ashkaraz, as well as an announcement that she would be marrying His Majesty, Tariq ibn Ishak Al Naziri.

Typing it felt unreal, as if it was happening to someone else, and a burst of homesickness made her wish for a phone call and the sound of her father's voice to steady her. But when she asked Amirah if a phone call was possible she was advised that it was forbidden.

At first she was merely annoyed, but as the day went on, with yet more beauty treatments that included being poked and prodded and then a fitting session for a wedding gown that involved being swathed in yards of white silk, Charlotte's annoyance soon turned to anger.

Everything was new and strange, and it was going to take her a while to get used to her new position in life. All she wanted was the sound of a familiar voice. Some reassurance that she was doing the right thing. That wasn't too much to ask, was it?

She'd already asked Amirah to beg the Sheikh for special dispensation for a call, especially since she had no idea when or even if she'd see her father again, but apparently 'forbidden' really meant forbidden.

There would be no phone calls for her.

Charlotte tried very hard to force her anger away, but for some reason she couldn't ignore it. Nor was it helped by her homesickness. And by the time the afternoon rolled around her emotions had begun to bubble away inside her like a saucepan full of water boiling on a stove.

She'd been preparing for a visit to the historic and apparently very beautiful palace baths, but as her anger had risen she'd decided to find the Sheikh first and tell him exactly what she thought of his phone call ban.

Over the past few days a steady stream of clothing had arrived in the suite—not only traditional robes, but expensive designer dresses, tailored trousers and shirts, blouses, as well several pairs of jeans and T-shirts. There was also underwear, silk and lace, in various pretty colours, which she'd tried to ignore because she felt strange about it. It was even stranger to wear the clothing and find that it was all the right size and fitted her perfectly.

In amongst the items she'd unearthed a very lovely bikini that had jewels sewn all over it. She had no idea if the jewels were real—if so, then the bikini wasn't very practical for swimming in, although it wasn't practical even if they weren't real—but still, it was the only bathing suit she had, and if she wanted to go to the baths, then that was what she'd have to wear.

Amirah had laughed and told her not to be so silly. Bathing naked was the done thing, and no one would bother her once it was known that the sheikha-to-be was bathing there. But there was no way she was bathing naked in public, so she pulled on the bikini, then a gauzy silver robe over the top of it, and, belting the robe around her waist, she went in search of the Sheikh.

However, he was nowhere to be found, and people seemed reluctant to tell her where he was. After half an hour's fruitless search, even more furious than she'd been initially, Charlotte decided to visit the baths anyway and look for him later. Certainly that would give her some time to cool off, and that was a good thing when it came to asking for a favour.

Except as she approached the arched entrance to the baths she saw two black-robed guards standing on either side of the door. She knew who they were now: the sheikh's personal guards. Which, of course, meant that he was inside.

Her temper was not improved by the news, since she'd been hoping to calm down in some peace and quiet. And a part of her was very tempted to simply turn around and go back to her rooms. But running away wouldn't get her a phone call, so she steeled herself, opening her mouth to demand entrance.

Yet before she'd even managed to get a word out, the guards stood aside for her, their faces impassive.

Charlotte shut her mouth with a snap, lifted her chin, and swept on past them, entering an echoing, humid space with high arches and columns set around a huge tiled pool. The walls had the same beautiful tiles as the rest of the palace, though these were in gorgeous shades of blue, and steam wreathed the huge columns that lined the edges of the pool. Light drifted down from the ceiling through hidden windows, illuminating the baths with a diffuse light.

A man was swimming in the pool, his stroke clean and powerful, his large muscular body moving through the water with all the deadly grace of a shark.

It was him. The Sheikh.

An unexpected shiver rippled through her, and the anger sitting in the pit of her stomach twisted strangely. There was something about him she couldn't take her eyes off, and instead of calling to interrupt him she found herself standing at the edge of the pool and watching him swim instead.

But he must have noticed her anyway, because his stroke slowed and gradually he came to a stop, standing up in the water and raising a hand to push his wet black hair back from his face.

And Charlotte realised she'd made a grievous error.

She very carefully hadn't thought of that night beside the fountain, losing herself instead in the tasks he'd set her over the past couple of days. Hadn't thought about the feelings he'd evoked, the anger and the strange sense of excitement as he'd brushed that strawberry over her lips, the fierce rush of adrenaline as he'd stared at her, challenge burning in his golden eyes.

And if he had accidentally found his way into her thoughts she'd distanced herself from him, turning him into the tall, dark and intimidating Sheikh instead, swathed in his robes of state. Safely removed from her by his position.

Yet it wasn't the robed Sheikh who stood in front of her now, but a man.

A magnificent, completely beautiful man.

Water streamed down his powerful body, outlining every perfect muscle from his wide shoulders to his broad chest, to the chiselled lines of his abs. His bronzed skin was marked here and there by scars, but nothing could detract from the fact that he was a work of art. There was not an ounce of fat on him and he was muscled like a Greek god, radiating the same sense of arrogant power.

And yet although he might look very much a man in the pool right now, every soaking wet inch of him was a king.

The distance she'd put between herself and her feelings felt abruptly tenuous, fraying as the diffuse light ran over his magnificent body. Her skin prickled with an undeniable heat. Her hands itched, as if she wanted to touch him, to see if he felt as hard and as smooth and as hot as he looked, forcing her to fold her arms and tuck her hands firmly into her armpits to stop herself from reaching for him.

'Good morning, Miss Devereaux.'

His deep, dark voice echoed in the tiled space and his golden stare caught hers, a knowing look in it.

'Have you come to join me for a swim?'

The prickling heat crept up her neck, warmed her cheeks, and she was very conscious that the humid air of the pool was making the gauzy fabric of her robes stick to her skin, and that all she had on beneath it was the silly, impractical little jewelled bikini.

'No,' she said stoutly, folding her arms tighter across her chest, determined not to let him get to her. 'I'm here to discuss the fact that you won't allow me a phone call with my father before he leaves.'

'Really?'

His gaze dropped down her body in a way that made her face feel even hotter.

'And yet you seem to be wearing the bikini I had sent to you.'

Damn him for noticing.

Charlotte shifted uncomfortably, felt the tiles warm and slick beneath her feet. 'Yes, well… you're already in here and I prefer to swim by myself. Now, about that phone—'

'Do not let me stop you,' he murmured. 'I would hate for you not to enjoy the water because of me.'

Another tiny shiver swept over her at the silky note in his voice and she couldn't seem to drag her gaze from the way the light fell on his wet skin.

Heavens, what was wrong with her? This man was a stranger to her, she'd barely even spoken to him, and yet all she could think about was what he would feel like beneath her fingers.

You're attracted to him. A good thing, considering he's going to be your husband.

She felt breathless at the thought, which irritated her, because she didn't want to feel anything at all about the man who'd essentially kidnapped her and was now holding her prisoner in his country.

'I don't want to swim right now,' she said primly. 'I want to talk about this phone call.'

Something gleamed in his eyes. 'Come into the pool, *ya amar*, and we will discuss it.'

Oh, she recognised that look. She'd seen it before, that night beside the fountain, when he'd told her she was to marry him. Fierce challenge. A dare.

And, much to her annoyance, she could feel a part of herself wanting to answer that challenge, to surprise him, make him see that she wasn't just his prisoner but a force to be reckoned with.

A stupid thing to want when she didn't care what he thought of her.

She didn't want to swim. She didn't want to get anywhere near him. And she wasn't his 'most beautiful', so he could stop calling her that too.

All she wanted was to talk to her father on the phone—that was it.

'I have already told you I don't want to swim,' she said, knowing she sounded sulky and yet unable to help it. 'Why do you keep insisting?'

'Because I have been neglecting you for the past couple of days.' The water rippled around his narrow hips as he moved closer. 'And I would like to catch up with what you have been doing.'

'I've been doing everything you asked me to do.' It seemed to take immense effort to keep her gaze on his face, not to look down and follow the muscled lines of his body. 'That's all.'

'Amirah tells me you have been diligent in your reading and an apt pupil in your language and protocol lessons.'

Charlotte shrugged, trying to ignore the way the light was moving over his chest as he breathed, his skin glistening. 'I like to study.'

He moved closer still and she couldn't help

herself. Her attention dropping down over him again and… Was he wearing swimming trunks?

She blinked and looked away, her face suddenly flaming.

No, he was not.

He's naked. He's standing in the water, naked.

Her pulse sounded loud in her ears—so loud it was a wonder he didn't hear it himself—and her mouth was bone-dry. Amirah had told her the custom was to swim naked, but Charlotte had never expected that to apply to the Sheikh himself. That she'd find him swimming naked and completely unashamed of the fact.

Not that he had anything to be ashamed about, from the looks of things.

Don't look at him, idiot.

That was a very good plan. Because the more she looked at him, the more breathless and unsteady she felt, and she didn't like it. Not one bit. She preferred to be in control of both herself and her feelings, not at their mercy.

Perhaps she'd simply pretend he was standing in front of her fully dressed and not…not…

'Is there something wrong?'

His voice was laced through with a fine thread

of amusement that scratched at her thin veneer of calm, threatening to crack it.

'No, of course not.' She steeled herself to meet his gaze again, determined not to let him see how he affected her. 'What makes you say that?'

'You are blushing very hard, Miss Devereaux.'

Oh, yes, he was very definitely amused, damn him.

'Why is that?'

Curse her pale skin. And curse him into the bargain.

Well, there was no point pretending now. Might as well give him the truth. 'Because you're naked, that's why. And, no, I'm very much *not* swimming with you. Not like that.'

'Why not?' One dark brow arched. 'Are you afraid?'

The question echoed off the tiled walls, and the deep vibration of his voice set something vibrating inside her too.

Was he making fun of her? Or was this about something more?

Oh, but she knew the answer to that. He was challenging her, pure and simple, and the part of her that wanted very much to answer that challenge was getting stronger. Because wouldn't it be satisfying to set his arrogance back on its heels?

Using your fear, though. That's a clichéd move.

Yes, it was—which meant that the only real response was to stay cool and calm, turn around and walk out.

Yet she didn't. She stayed where she was, rooted to the spot, angry and getting angrier. At herself for her conflicting emotions and at him for making her feel this way. Because it was definitely his fault. She'd never had any trouble controlling her anger before—never had anyone get under her skin the way he was doing right now.

And the real problem was that the longer she stood there, the more she revealed—and he knew it. In fact, he was looking at her now as if he could see her every thought, knew her every feeling, knew that she was afraid and that he was the cause. And he liked it.

'I will not touch you,' he said softly. 'If that is what you are afraid of.'

Oh, yes, he could see her fear. Bloody man.

Her jaw felt tight, aching. 'I am *not* afraid.'

'Get in, then. And we will discuss your phone call.'

She didn't want to. But she couldn't stand there doing nothing any longer.

Before she could think better of it Charlotte moved to the edge of the pool.

Then dived straight in.

CHAPTER SIX

TARIQ HAD NOT expected that. He'd been bait-
ing her, admittedly, and it was probably unfair
of him, but she'd turned up during his private
swimming time, her silver-blue eyes glowing
with anger, wearing a gauzy piece of nothing he
could see straight through and the tiny jewelled
bikini he'd provided for her on a whim, and…
Well, he was a man. And she was very much a
woman.

If he thought about it, he'd no doubt find it a
little disturbing, how affected he was by her.

But he'd decided not to think about it.

Her vulnerability was the issue, not her anger,
and with her standing there arguing with him,
the transparent robe clinging to her small cur-
vaceous figure and all that silvery hair curling
in the humidity of the baths, it hadn't seemed a
bad thing to indulge his urge to push her, bait

her just a little. Stoke her anger to see how hot it flared and whether she would burn along with it.

And indeed she had—beautifully, as it turned out.

Her response to him was all he could have hoped for, and he very much liked how uncomfortable his nakedness had made her. Because it was obvious why she was uncomfortable, and it wasn't due to her not liking his body. He knew when a woman wanted him, and his pretty little fiancée very much did, whether she was aware of it or not.

Still, he'd expected to have to drag out some more ultimatums before she finally got in the pool with him. And even then he'd thought she might slip in quietly, perhaps a little hesitantly.

He hadn't thought she'd dive right in, barely making a splash.

She came to the surface, water coursing down her body, the gauzy robe now completely transparent and sticking like a second skin to her lush curves. With her hair lying silky and wet over her shoulders, and water drops caught on her lashes, she looked like a mermaid.

His body tightened, hardening as she lifted

her arms to push her hair back. Her breasts rose with the movement, and the jewels on her bikini top glittered only slightly less brightly than her sapphire eyes as she met his gaze.

She was all challenge now, no longer calm and prim, the way she had been on the edge of the pool, and he felt something in him wanting to push her even harder, to see exactly what she was made of.

Because he had a feeling it was of stronger stuff than he'd initially anticipated. She'd been shocked at the ultimatum he'd presented her with the night he'd given her dinner, but then she'd got angry, giving him a glimpse of steel, and he'd very much liked that.

'So,' she said, holding out her hands. 'As you can see, I am now in the water. Can we have a conversation about my phone call now?'

Perhaps she didn't know the effect she presented in this moment—all pale, gleaming skin, her every curve highlighted by the gems on her swimsuit. Because if she had she might have requested more from him than a mere phone call. But plainly she didn't, and that was just as well since he might have given it to her.

She was a such a pretty, pretty thing.

And in addition to her steel he'd also had a glimpse of her passion that night beside the fountain, and he wanted to test it. Wanted to see if that passion truly did extend to him. Because her desire was going to be fairly crucial when it came to the provision of an heir; he would never force himself on an unwilling bride.

He'd held that strawberry out towards her, a challenge for her to accept, and accept it she had. He'd taken advantage, brushing the strawberry over her luscious mouth, watching her eyes grow round and then glow bright. Watching as her small white teeth had sunk into the flesh of the berry, taking a bite. When he'd withdrawn his hand he'd allowed his fingers to brush her lower lip, and it had been just as soft and silky as it had looked.

The memory of that mouth had taunted him for the past two days, no matter how many meetings and other duties he'd immersed himself in, and he couldn't seem to stop looking at it now. It was just as full as it had been that night, just as pink, and now sheened lightly with water.

Perhaps he needed to test her again, push her further. See how receptive she was so he knew what he'd be dealing with come their wedding night.

Slowly, he moved over to where she stood, then stopped in front of her. She tipped her head back to look at him, folding her arms again, but he saw the movement of her throat as she swallowed and noted the flicker of apprehension in her eyes as he came close.

He'd seen that same apprehension that night beside the fountain, but he'd put it down to shock. He had, after all, delivered an ultimatum with which she hadn't been at all happy. However, it surely wasn't shock now, so what could it be? She liked his body—that wasn't the issue—so it had to be something else. But what?

'I thought you said you were not afraid of me,' he murmured.

She blinked. Clearly she hadn't expected him to notice. 'I'm not.'

'But you are afraid?'

'N-no.'

The stutter was slight, but he caught it, narrowing his gaze and studying her more intently. 'Do not lie to me, Charlotte.'

She shifted in the water as he said her name, as if the sound of it affected her in some way.

'Well, okay. I suppose I am a little…apprehensive. But that's only because you're not wearing anything.'

'I will be your husband,' he pointed out. 'My not wearing anything is something you will have to get used to.'

Her blush deepened. The line of her shoulders was tense, and he had the odd urge to put his hands on her and stroke that tension away, ease her fear. But that would set a dangerous precedent, and not one he could afford.

And besides, he had the sense that it wasn't actually his nakedness that was the problem.

He took another experimental step towards her, watching as her eyes widened and her mouth opened slightly. And then something else flickered to life in the deep blue of her gaze.

Oh, she was bothered by him—of that he had no doubt. But it wasn't because she was afraid of him.

'So,' she said, quickly and sharply, as if she were using the words to stop him in his tracks. 'What do you want for a phone call?'

Momentarily distracted, he did stop. 'What do you mean?'

'You're very fond of ultimatums. *"Marry me*

or your father stays here. Get in the pool if you want to discuss a phone call.'" Her chin lifted even higher. 'So now I'm in the pool, what do you want in return for giving me that call? Because I can sense an ultimatum coming already, believe me.'

He might have found fault with the accusing note in her voice had he not already decided that she was using the phone call issue as a distraction. He also knew what she was trying to distract him from. But, unfortunately for her, it wasn't going to work. Since he'd decided on marriage securing the succession was going to be important, and he couldn't leave anything to chance.

Such as her being bothered by her own response to him.

'What is disturbing you, *ya amar*?' He took another step closer. 'Tell me the truth so we can discuss it.'

'The phone call—'

'It is not the phone call,' he interrupted flatly, taking yet another step, until mere inches separated them. 'You are afraid, and I do not think it is me you are afraid of, but yourself.'

She hadn't moved, yet her tension was obvious as her head tipped back so she could look up at him. The colour of her eyes had darkened and her mouth was slightly open, the pulse at the base of her throat racing.

'I…' she said hoarsely. 'I don't know what you're talking about.'

'I think you do.' He reached out and slid a careful hand behind her head, pushing his fingers through her wet hair and cradling the back of her skull in his palm.

She stiffened, and he could feel the tension in her neck, see it in the awkward way she was trying to hold herself away from him.

'Your Majesty…'

'"Your Majesty" is unnecessary. You may call me Tariq.'

Her throat moved as she swallowed, her gaze pinned to his. 'I'm happy with Your Majesty.'

Stubborn girl.

'You cannot call your husband *Your Majesty*,' he said, amused. 'Say my name, Charlotte.'

He stroked his thumb over the tight muscles at her nape, watching as her eyes darkened even further, her pupils dilating into black. Oh, yes, she was certainly responsive to him, and it was exactly the kind of response he'd been hoping for.

'T-Tariq.'

His name was soft and smoky sounding, the slight stutter of it somehow erotic.

Ah, perfect.

He could feel himself harden, his own pulse beginning to ramp up. The slow melt of her resistance was unexpectedly seductive. Going slowly and carefully had never appealed to him much before, but he could certainly see the allure now.

'That's better.' He drew her close, so they were almost touching, continuing to stroke the back of her neck, soothing her. 'You know, do you not, that wanting one's husband is perfectly acceptable?'

She was breathing very fast, her gaze dropping to his mouth and staying there. 'I… I don't want you.'

He nearly smiled at the obviousness of the lie. 'Of course you do not. That is why you have not told me to stop.'

Charlotte drew in another shaky little breath, yet her gaze didn't move from his mouth and her head lay heavy in the palm of his hand, the tension bleeding out of her muscles completely.

'I should.'

'Why?' He searched her flushed face. 'Physical desire is nothing to be afraid of.'

She gave him a brief, fleeting look before she looked away again. 'I wouldn't know. I've… never felt it before.'

So… All of this was new to her. Perhaps she was even a virgin…

A deep possessiveness he hadn't known was inside him stirred, along with a satisfaction that would have disturbed him if he'd thought about it in any depth.

But he didn't want to think about it in any depth, so he didn't.

'You feel it now.' He didn't make it a question.

Her lashes fell, her gaze once more going to his mouth, as if she couldn't help herself. She didn't speak. But then she didn't need to. He knew the answer already.

Of course she felt it.

'Say it again,' he murmured. 'My name.'

'Tariq…'

The word had barely left her lips before he'd bent and covered them with his in a feather-light kiss. A mere brush across her mouth. To taste her and tempt her. To test their undeniable physical chemistry.

She went very still, her body trembling.

He'd intended to end the kiss almost as soon as it had started, thinking that would be sufficient, and yet he found he couldn't pull away, that something inside him was catching fire.

He touched his tongue to her bottom lip instead, tracing the line of it the way he'd traced it with that strawberry, and she trembled even harder. Then her lips were softening, opening for him, and he couldn't stop himself from deepening the kiss, allowing his tongue to sweep in and taste her.

Oh, so sweet… Like that strawberry. Like honey. Like the late-summer wine that came from the vineyards in the valley to the south.

He spread his hand out on the back of her head, his fingers pushing into her hair, holding her still as he kissed her more deeply, chasing that sweetness.

She gave a little throaty moan. The sound made all the blood in his body rush to a certain part of his anatomy, and all of a sudden the kiss turned hot—far hotter than he'd intended.

This was supposed to be a test. For her, not for him. And yet he found that he was the one on the edge of control.

He wanted her robe gone. Her bikini gone. He wanted her naked and up against the wall of the pool. He wanted to be inside her.

Her hands touched his chest, her fingers pure electricity on his skin.

If you do not stop now, that is exactly what will happen.

And it must not. He knew what happened when he didn't control himself…when he let passion get the better of him. Distance—that was what his father had taught him. Distance and detachment. And that was not what was happening now.

It took every ounce of will he had, but he managed it, tearing his mouth from hers and letting her go.

She was staring at him in shock, her mouth full and red from the kiss, her eyes round as saucers and dark as midnight.

'I will arrange your phone call,' he said brusquely.

Then he turned around and left the pool before she could say a word.

'I don't like it, Charlotte.'

Her father's voice sounded cracked and tinny down the phone.

'I don't like it at all.'

Charlotte gripped the phone Tariq had handed to her hard and tried to ignore her future husband, standing on the other side of the desk, his face impassive.

He'd been as good as his word in arranging the call, though he'd offered no explanation for his sudden change of heart. She thought it might have something to do with what had happened between them in the baths the day before, but she wasn't sure.

She was trying *very* hard not to think about that herself. Though it was difficult when he'd insisted on remaining in the room while she spoke to her father, watching her with his intent golden stare.

'It's okay, Dad,' she said, trying to be reassuring. 'Like I was saying, we met and…f-fell in love, and he asked me to marry him. And I said yes.'

'But it's only been three days,' her father pointed out, sounding cross.

'Isn't that how long it took you to decide to marry Mum?'

Her parents had had a mad, passionate, whirlwind romance—at least that was what her father had said, always bitterly—followed by a quick wedding. And then, years later, an acrimonious divorce.

With her in the middle.

She was suddenly even more conscious of Tariq, just on the other side of the desk, staring at her intensely. His presence was intimidating, pressing in on her, making her skin prickle with heat at the memory of his mouth on hers, the feeling of his hand cradling the back of her head, his body tall and powerful and so achingly close.

Speaking of mad and passionate...

That had been her yesterday, at the baths. Her heartbeat had been frantic, her skin too tight and too hot. She'd been overwhelmed by him, by the taste of him—something indescribable that reminded her of dense, rich, hot chocolate. Sweet and decadent and dark.

She should have stopped him, but when he'd touched her she hadn't even been able to remember why it was wrong to want him anyway. He'd told her that physical desire wasn't anything to be afraid of and in that moment, with the way he'd held her and the gentleness with which he'd explored her, fear had been the last thing she'd felt. All she'd been conscious of was her hunger. For him.

Her pulse was beating hard now, almost drowning out her father's voice.

'Yes, that's true,' he was saying. 'But look what happened there. That woman ruined my life and nearly destroyed my career, while she got to swan off with her divorce settlement, footloose and fancy-free.'

Meaning without the millstone of her daughter hanging around her neck, presumably, though Charlotte didn't ask him that. She knew his thoughts on the matter. If she hadn't got so afraid and run off during one of their more bitter arguments, staying out the whole night while her parents called the police, trying to find her, her mother might have continued to fight the custody battle and would probably have won.

But her mother hadn't continued to fight. She'd deemed Charlotte too much of a problem and left her with her father.

'Well,' her father went on crossly, not waiting for her to speak, 'I suppose if that's what you want to do, then that's what you want to do. But now I'll have to find myself a new bloody assistant.'

So he might never see his daughter again and all he could think about was hiring a new assistant?

Did you expect it to be different? For him to care?

No—and that was the sad thing. She didn't. He'd never made a secret of how unhappy he'd been when he was granted full custody of her, how she'd limited him in terms of his career, and how if she hadn't gone running off that night things would have been different.

The fact that she'd tried very hard *not* to be an impediment to his career as a kid, and then as an adult—had actively tried to help him with it, in fact—didn't seem to register.

'Sorry, Dad,' she said, not knowing what else to say. The pressure of Tariq's gaze was like a weight, pressing down on her.

'Can't be helped, I suppose,' her father muttered. 'Look, I'd better go. These soldiers look like they're ready to get rid of me. Speak soon.'

The call disconnected.

He doesn't care and you know it.

Her eyes prickled, which made her angry. Because, yes, she did know it. She always had. The professor resented her, so why she kept trying to change his mind about her she had no idea.

He's all you have—that's why.

But that didn't bear thinking about—especially not with Tariq still staring at her so intently. She didn't want him knowing how little she was valued by the only important person in her life, and she especially didn't want him seeing her tears.

So she swallowed down the lump in her throat, blinked the moisture from her eyes and handed him back the phone. 'Thank you,' she said, pleased that her voice at least sounded level. 'I don't think there will be any repercussions for you.'

He took the phone and slid it back into his pocket, but his gaze didn't leave her face. 'What did he say to you?'

So he'd picked up on her upset. Wonderful.

'I don't think that's any of your business.'

'You will be my wife soon,' he said flatly. 'Everything you do is my business.'

There was a stillness to him, an intensity that unnerved her. Though that wasn't the only unnerving thing about him. In suit trousers and a black business shirt open at the neck, displaying bronze skin and the beat of a strong pulse, he had a charisma that was undeniable.

She found herself staring at that pulse and thinking about what it would be like if she brushed her mouth over it. What his skin would taste like. What he would do if she did that...

'Charlotte,' he said softly. 'Up here.'

She jerked her gaze up to his, her cheeks hot with embarrassment. Because of course he'd know exactly what she was thinking—like he had in the baths yesterday. She'd tried to hide it, tried to distract him with her request for a phone call, but he hadn't been deflected. He'd been relentless, getting the truth out of her whether she wanted to give it to him or not.

You liked giving it to him.

The taste of him was suddenly in her mouth, the memory of his lips on hers scorching.

'He said nothing,' she murmured thickly, trying to shove the memories from her head. 'Just that he'd have to get a new assistant.'

The gold of Tariq's eyes was molten, the heat in them like the desert sun. As if he was angry. But she couldn't imagine why he would be.

'That is all?'

'Yes.'

'It upset you?'

'Of course it upset me.' She tried to keep her voice level. 'He's my father and now I'll never see him again.'

Tariq's gaze narrowed. 'I do not think that is why you are upset.'

But she didn't want to have this particular conversation. She felt too raw, too uncertain. There was the pain of her father's dismissal and her own anger, as well as the press of that unfamiliar hunger every time she looked at the Sheikh, standing behind his desk. The memory of his kiss still burned in her mind and she didn't want it there.

She looked away. 'Perhaps we could talk about this at a different time? I have to—'

She didn't hear him move, but he must have done because suddenly one large hand was cupping her cheek, his thumb brushing over her skin. 'You hoped for more from him?'

Her heart was beating loudly in her ears again and his body was inches away. His palm against her skin was hot, and part of her wanted to jerk away while another part wanted to lean into his touch. It had been such a long time since anyone had touched her quite like this. A long time since anyone had been interested in her feelings.

'Yes, I did,' she said, not sure why she was telling him this when she'd been so determined not to. 'I hoped he might be upset that he wouldn't see me again rather than because he'd have to get a new assistant.'

His thumb brushed her cheek again and she didn't want to look at him. Because he was too close and that raw feeling in her chest wouldn't go away. Those golden eyes of his would see her vulnerability all too easily, and he'd know how badly her father's easy dismissal had hurt.

And then he'll want to know why.

Yes, he would. And she didn't want to tell him.

'He knows that he will not see you again?' Tariq asked.

'I told him.' She swallowed, gathering herself, then pulled away from his touch and forced a smile on her face. 'He's absent-minded a lot of the time, so I'm not sure he listened. Anyway, that's that, I suppose. What made you change your mind about giving me the call?'

Tariq's hand dropped and he remained where he was, making no move towards her. But he continued to study her, his gaze unsettling in its intensity. 'Maybe it was your kiss,' he murmured.

And any relief she felt that he'd dropped the subject of her father vanished as heat filled her at the reminder of what had happened the day before. She was conscious once again of the throb of hunger down low inside her.

The space between them suddenly felt electric, crackling with a strange static charge that had her breath catching.

'If you are thinking that our marriage will be in name only, you are wrong, Charlotte,' he went on, his voice even lower and deeper. 'You do understand that, do you not?'

Don't pretend you don't know what he's talking about.

Her mouth was dry and she couldn't seem to find any air. Because of course she knew what he was talking about—and it was something she'd conveniently not been thinking about. At least not until he'd kissed her.

He meant sex.

And he meant that he intended to have sex with her.

Heat swept through her, burning everything in

its path, and she had to turn away so he wouldn't see the way her face flamed.

'Of course I understand,' she said automatically. 'Goodness, look at the time. I have to—'

'I would not want there to be any misunderstanding.' There was no mistaking the intent in his words, or the dark hint of sensuality that threaded through his tone. 'We have a certain… chemistry, *ya amar*. And I fully intend to explore that as thoroughly as possible.'

A certain chemistry…

He wants you.

The thought blazed in her brain for a second, bright as neon. She hadn't thought about how she might affect him—mainly because she'd been too busy thinking about how he affected her. But he'd kissed her for a long time yesterday, and the kiss had soon turned hotter, deeper. He'd become demanding, and his grip on her had tightened, his body responding. And then he'd let her go abruptly, with something blazing in his eyes that had looked like anger.

She hadn't thought about why he might have been angry—hadn't thought at all about why he'd let her go either. She'd tried to put it out of her mind entirely.

But maybe she should think about it. Maybe she had was some power she'd never expected to find.

'I see,' she said slowly, turning over the discovery in her head.

'Do you? Look at me, Charlotte.'

There was no resisting the command and she didn't, turning back to him, her gaze clashing with his. And for a moment she was back in the desert, with the sun a hammer-blow of heat, crushing her with its force.

'Tell me you understand,' he said.

She met the ferocity in his eyes, for some reason feeling less vulnerable than she had a moment ago. The knowledge that she wasn't without power here was giving her a courage she hadn't expected to feel.

'I understand.'

He stared back at her for a long, uncounted moment. Then he turned around and went back to the desk.

'I suggest you do some research on the marriage customs of Ashkaraz,' he said, sitting down. 'Amirah will show you which books to read in the library. Some of them you should find quite interesting.'

His attention was on his computer screen now, which obviously meant that she was dismissed.

But that was good.

She had a lot to think about.

CHAPTER SEVEN

TARIQ HAD NEVER been one for weddings, and he hadn't been particularly interested in the preparations for his own. Not when it was the wedding night he couldn't stop thinking about. To a disturbing degree.

Then again, focusing on physical pleasure had been better than going over his behaviour in his office the day she'd spoken to her father, and how he'd given in to the disturbing urge to comfort her.

He still didn't understand why he had, or why the need to do so had hit him so strongly. All he'd seen in her blue eyes was a flash of pain. And then she wouldn't tell him what the problem was, so he'd gone around the desk, reaching for her and cupping her cheek before he'd been able to think better of it.

A mistake.

He couldn't afford slips like that and he knew it. So for the past week he'd distanced himself from her, busying himself with his duties as well as with preparations for the wedding. And there had been a lot to prepare, since he wanted the whole business over and done with as quickly as possible.

As per royal custom, the ceremony itself was being held on the palace steps, in full view of his people.

Charlotte was robed in gauzy white silk, embroidered all over with silver and belted at the waist with a silver sash that had long sparkling tassels falling almost to her ankles. Her hair was loose, as was also the custom, and gleaming in the sun, and she wore a simple platinum circlet around her brow, with one of Ashkaraz's rare blue diamonds in the centre.

Her face was very pale as she appeared, and it went even paler as she saw the assembled crowds. But she didn't hesitate as she was led to where he stood, alongside the officiant who would conduct the ceremony.

His people hadn't been given much time to come to terms with their Sheikh marrying a foreigner, but as soon as Charlotte appeared they gave her a hearty cheer. Apparently they were as susceptible to a white wedding gown as he was.

And he was.

He couldn't take his eyes off her as she joined him on the steps, all silvery and white and bright as the moon. Beautiful, too, and delicate. He hadn't thought that would affect him, but it did.

And as she recited the complicated vows without a single hesitation he was conscious of that dark satisfaction sweeping through him again—the same feeling he'd had in the baths that day. A feeling he'd not experienced about a person before. Not when his life had been all about feeling nothing for individual people at all.

It was the whole that was important—at least that was what his father had taught him. His country and his people were what he ought to have uppermost in his mind. He did not need to concern himself with specifics.

Yet he was aware, as her vows were being said, that he was feeling something very specific now—and that feeling was centred entirely on a person.

Mine, the feeling told him. *She is mine.*

He hadn't had anything that was his before—not one single thing. All of it had been for 'the Sheikh' rather than the man. All except Catherine. And even she had been his father's first. Never his.

But Charlotte was. Charlotte was his completely.

He felt almost savage as the vows were completed and their hands were joined. Her delicate fingers were cool in his, and he was already thankful for the traditions of Ashkarazi royal marriage that required the bride and groom to retire immediately after the wedding to an oasis in the south, sacred to the royal family, for three days, to ensure the getting of an heir.

It should have been disturbing to feel this intensely about a woman, but it had been some time since he'd taken his pleasure, so it was no wonder that was all he could think about.

After the vows and rings were exchanged, and the people had cheered their new sheikha, Tariq wasted no time in taking Charlotte's elbow and whisking her from the palace to the helipad, where his helicopter stood ready to take them to the oasis.

She gave him a startled look as his guards fell into step around them and he urged her along the path to the helipad. 'Where are we going? Isn't there a reception or a party? I read that—'

'You read, presumably, about what happens directly after a royal wedding here?'

She flushed, the colour standing out beautifully on her pale skin. 'Oh, the sacred oasis. Of course.'

The shy way she said it only made the savage feeling inside him grow more intense, and it was a good thing that there was no more opportunity for talk as they came to the helicopter.

He helped her into it, bundling the long white skirts of her wedding robes around her, and a few minutes later they were in the air, soaring high over the city of Kharan and then following the long valley down to where the oasis was situated.

It was about an hour from the palace, in isolated, rocky desert, and surrounding the bright green and blue jewel of the oasis were palm trees and grasses.

The chopper took them down, and when it had landed Tariq helped Charlotte out. Palace staff had spent the last day or so setting up the tents that contained all the facilities both of them would need for three days alone, and a couple were still there to help unload their luggage from the helicopter.

Charlotte was silent as Tariq led her over to

a low divan set under some shady palms, then went back to help with the unloading of the helicopter. He didn't have to do it, but he couldn't sit still waiting for everyone to leave. He wanted them gone, and quickly.

Another couple of minutes later and the chopper was rising into the air and heading back up the valley to Kharan, leaving Tariq finally alone with his bride.

She'd remained sitting on the divan under the palms in a pool of white and silver silk, her hands clasped in her lap, her silvery hair loose down her back. A smile curved her mouth as he stalked over to her, though he could see it was forced.

'So,' she said breathlessly, 'I guess this is where we are. In the oasis.'

He stopped in front of her, studying her face. A fine sheen of sweat gleamed on her brow, because it was only late afternoon and still suffocatingly hot, despite their proximity to the water. It wouldn't cool down till well after dark.

But he didn't think it was entirely the heat that was making her sweat.

She was nervous.

His own need was beating inside him like a

drum, and the urge to pick her up and take her to the bedroom tent was almost overpowering.

Why the impatience? You have plenty of time.

That was true. They did have three days, after all. And maybe it would even do him good to practise some restraint—especially after the incident in the baths when he'd almost forgotten himself. He was supposed to remain detached, after all.

Yet he didn't feel detached now. He wanted her skin damp and slippery from something other than the heat and her silver-blue eyes full of fire. He wanted more of the kisses he'd taken from her, and the taste of her latent passion on his tongue. He wanted to rouse it, stoke it. Make it burn for him and only for him.

And why not? She was his wife now. And he'd told her that their marriage would not be in name only. She had always known what would be expected.

But it was not her choice to marry you—remember that. You railroaded her into it.

He didn't know why he was thinking about that now. Not when his body was hardening, desire and possessiveness coursing through him. And it wouldn't change the fact that although she might not have had a choice about the marriage, she still wanted him. He hadn't forgotten the throaty moan she'd made when he'd kissed her in the baths, or how her mouth had opened beneath his, wanting more.

Her attention was on him, she was watching him, and she must know what he was thinking because he could see that familiar flicker of apprehension in her eyes. But the heat he remembered from the baths was burning there too.

Oh, yes, she wanted him. But she was afraid of it.

'Do not look so frightened, *ya amar*,' he said, a rough edge creeping into his voice. 'I have already told you that I will not hurt you.'

'I'm not frightened.' Her hands twisted in her lap, her gaze darting around, looking everywhere but at him. 'Could we perhaps go for a swim first? I'm rather hot.'

His patience thinned, irritation coiling with the desire twisting inside him. 'You are lying, Charlotte. And I have told you already that will not work. Not with me. And definitely not now we are about to consummate our marriage.'

Her lashes fell. 'I'm not lying.'

'Then why are your hands twisting in your lap? And why will you not look directly at me?'

She was already flushed with heat and now her cheeks went even pinker. With a deliberate movement, she unclenched her hands, laying them flat on the white silk of her skirts. Then her lashes rose and she looked at him.

'There. Is that better?'

'No,' he said impatiently. 'Do not play with me.'

'I'm not playing with you,' she shot back, and there was the slight edge of temper rising in her voice. 'I'm only trying to—'

'And do not try to placate me either.'

He didn't want to stand there arguing with her. He wanted to take her to bed. But her nervousness and vulnerability were making his chest tight and he didn't like it.

Detachment—that was what he had to strive for. Detachment and isolation. Not being concerned with another person's feelings.

'I'm *not* trying to placate you.' Charlotte pushed herself to her feet, her cheeks red, her blue eyes full of anger. 'I'm nervous, if you must know. I told you the truth in the baths when I said I hadn't felt anything physically for a man before. I haven't. But I feel something for you and I… I don't know what do.' She stopped, took a breath, and glanced away. 'I'm a virgin. And I… I don't want to disappoint you.'

He went very still.

She is yours completely.

He'd suspected she was innocent already, and yet the possessiveness that deepened and broadened in response to her confession was almost shocking.

Yes, she was his. Completely. And why she would think he might find that disappointing was anyone's guess.

'You should have told me,' he growled. 'That is something I need to know. And as for disappointing me…' He stared hard into her flushed face. 'Why would you think that?'

Her jaw tightened, her discomfort obvious, but she didn't look away this time. 'You didn't choose me because you wanted me, Tariq. You chose me because I was convenient.'

'But you must know that I want you. Surely that kiss in the baths told you that?'

'That doesn't change the fact that you wouldn't have married me if I hadn't accidentally wandered into your kingdom.'

'No, I would not.' He couldn't lie; it was the truth. 'But what does that have to do with anything? Do you want me to feel something for you? Is that what you are asking?'

Emotions flickered over her face, but they were gone so fast he couldn't tell what they were.

Then her gaze dropped again, her shoulders drooping. 'No,' she said. 'That's not what I'm asking. Forget I said anything.'

It was not what he'd planned. And it wasn't what he wanted. That tightness in his chest was back, and he didn't know why the sight of her looking so defeated affected him the way it did. It reminded him of the expression on her face that day in his office, during her father's phone call, the bright flash of hurt.

Which shouldn't matter to him. Her self-doubt had nothing to do with him. And yet he couldn't let it go.

He reached out, took her chin in his hand and tilted her head up so her gaze met his. 'Do not change the subject. Answer me, Charlotte. Why do you think you would be a disappointment?'

'You…are stuck with me.' There was a catch in her voice. 'And let's just say that hasn't worked out well for me before.'

Her skin was so soft, so silky. He rubbed his thumb gently along her lower lip, unable to stop himself from touching her, the need inside him becoming even fiercer.

But this was too important to interrupt. 'Tell me,' he ordered quietly.

She let out a soft breath, her lashes falling again, the sunlight turning them to pure silver. 'My parents had a very bitter divorce. My mother decided not to contest custody so Dad ended up with me. He was not…happy about it. Said it would affect his career.'

Tariq frowned, staring down at her lovely face, conscious of yet another unwanted emotion threading through him: anger. On her behalf. Because what kind of father would say that to his child? What kind of father would make sure his child knew she wasn't wanted?

His own father had been strict, and Tariq had been so angry with him—yet Ishak had done what he had because he'd wanted Tariq to be the best king possible. Of course Tariq had ended up disappointing him in the end, but that hadn't been his father's fault. And he was making good now.

And so was she. Sacrificing her freedom in return for her father's. Making the best of marrying a complete stranger. Throwing herself into all the tasks he'd set her, learning his language and his customs without complaint.

She is trying. Like you are trying.

The need inside him twisted, deepened, ached. Became something more.

'Well, you are not a disappointment to me,' he said before he could stop himself. 'You are the opposite. You are beautiful and loyal and you have done what you could in a situation you did not choose and did not want. You are everything I want in a wife.'

There was something fearfully hopeful in her gaze as it searched his, as if she couldn't quite bring herself to believe him yet wanted to.

'But I'm not experienced. I don't know—'

Tariq put his thumb gently over her mouth, stopping the words. 'I do not need you to be experienced. I have enough experience for both of us. Now...' He paused, letting her see what burned inside him: the desire for her. 'I am tired of waiting, Charlotte. And I do not want to talk. What I want is to take you to bed.'

Her lips were soft and full beneath his thumb, the blue of her eyes darkening. There was already a sheen of perspiration on her skin and wisps of hair were sticking to her forehead—not a good thing when what he was planning to do to her would make her even hotter.

He frowned. 'Perhaps you do need cooling down first, though.'

'Oh, but I'm not—'

Decision made, he didn't wait for her to finish, dropping his hand and giving in to the need to get close to her by gathering her small, curvy figure in his arms.

She gave a soft gasp, but didn't protest, tipping her head back against his shoulder as his grip tightened, her eyes very blue in her flushed face.

'I thought you were tired of waiting?'

'Who says I will wait?' He began to stride through the palms, anticipation coiling inside him. 'A swim can involve all kinds of things.'

She blinked, obviously thinking about this. 'Oh. So you might…um…?'

'Consummate our marriage in the water?' he finished. 'I might.'

Judging by how hard he was right now, it might even be inevitable.

He didn't want to pause to undress her, so he walked straight into the oasis, wading out into the middle, still carrying her. The water was deliciously cool against his own hot skin, making his wedding robes stick to him, and as it flooded over her she gave a little gasp, wriggling against him.

'But I'm still dressed!'

'I realise that.' He moved deeper, until the water was at his chest and she was clutching at him, white silk floating all around her, her breathing fast at the shock of the water.

'But what about a swimsuit?'

'You do not need a swimsuit.'

Her weight in his arms was slight, her body warm, her hands gripping his robes tightly.

He glanced down at her, noting how her flush had receded. 'You are feeling cooler now?'

'Yes, much better, thank you.'

A crease appeared between her fair brows as she met his gaze. The water was lapping at her hair, making it float around her like fine silver thread.

'You're really quite kind, aren't you?'

He wasn't sure what went through him in that moment. It was a wave of something he wasn't familiar with. Almost as if he…liked what she'd said. Which was strange. Because he wasn't kind, and nor did he want to be. Kindness reminded him of mercy, of sympathy, of the soft feelings he associated with Catherine. Of his weakness when it came to his own emotions. Anger. Desire. Need.

But he wasn't going to think about those things.

Instead, he shoved away the warmth that threatened, concentrated instead on the desire burning like fire in his blood.

'No,' he said, adjusting his hold on her to reach for the silver belt at her waist. 'Kind is one thing I am not.'

And then he pulled hard, systematically beginning to strip her robes from her body.

CHAPTER EIGHT

TARIQ'S FINGERS ON her were firm as he stripped away her heavy, water-soaked robes, but it was the look on his face that made her breath catch.

His jaw was tight, tension radiated from him, and his features looked as if they'd been carved from granite. The only thing that wasn't hard and cold was his gaze, and a kind of molten intensity was burning in his eyes.

Burning in her too.

What had she said? That he was kind? He'd been kind to her that day she'd spoken to her father, and he'd been kind to her just before, underneath the palm trees, as nervousness and the strangeness of the whole day had got to her. As she'd been overwhelmed by the fact that she was now married to a king and that he was going to take her virginity, probably right where she stood.

He'd looked so stern, so forbidding as the helicopter had left. And the courage that had carried her through the wedding ceremony in front of seemingly the entire city had deserted her.

She'd tried to pretend she was fine, but suddenly, under his intimidating stare, all she'd felt was doubt. In herself, and in what was going to happen, and in the intensity of her own desire too.

It had only occurred to her then that, as much as she hadn't had a choice in their marriage, perhaps neither had he. He needed an heir, and he hadn't been able to choose a wife from his own people because he had an entire country he had to protect. And she'd been convenient.

Really, when she thought about it, it seemed he'd been stuck with her the same way her father had been stuck with her.

It shouldn't matter, but somehow it did. She didn't want him to be stuck with someone he was only going to be disappointed in—and she *would* end up disappointing him. She wasn't one of his people and she didn't speak his language. She didn't know his customs or what was expected of her.

She was a virgin with no experience whatsoever.

How could that not be disappointing to a man like him?

And yet he'd cupped her cheek in his hand, his gaze fierce with conviction. And he'd told her that she was beautiful. That she was loyal. That she was everything he'd hoped for.

He *was* kind, no matter what he said, and she didn't know why that made him so angry.

Maybe you should ask him?

She probably should—except now was not the right time, given the way he was looking at her, as if he wanted to eat her alive.

A shiver coursed through her and it had nothing to do with the water lapping around her. Even forbidding and hard, the impact of him was like a gut-punch. She'd felt it the moment she'd met him on the steps of the palace, just before the ceremony. He'd been dressed in white, as had she, but his robes had been embroidered with gold. The white had set off his inky black hair and his bronze skin, and the gold thread had struck sparks from the deep gold of his eyes as he'd looked at her.

And for a second she hadn't been able to breathe. Because he had been so…overwhelming. Beautiful, and strong, and powerful. So achingly charismatic. He had drawn every eye, commanded all the attention.

She found it difficult to breathe now, as he stripped the long-sleeved over-robe off her, let the water move silkily over her bare arms, then began to pull at the ties of the long sleeveless tunic she wore.

'What's wrong with being kind?' she asked, not knowing she was going to say it until it was out and then, given how his features hardened still further, regretting it.

'There is nothing wrong with being kind.'

He pulled off the tunic, then tugged down the long, loose trousers that she wore underneath.

'But you're angry.'

She stared up into his face, trying to figure out why a simple compliment should bother him quite so much, but his expression remained impassive. Again, except for his eyes. They burned brilliant gold.

'Now is not the time for conversation, *ya amar.*'

His voice was rough and full of authority, and she couldn't help shivering as his hands stroked up her bare legs, his palms hot against her skin in stark contrast to the cool water.

'I know, but—'

She stopped abruptly as his hand slid around her, deftly undoing the clasp of her white lace bra and stripping it from her. The water licked over her skin, making her nipples harden, and everything she'd been going to say vanished from her brain.

'But what?' His gaze dropped to her bare breasts, his eyes glittering, heat flaring higher in them.

And she couldn't think.

Couldn't even form one rational thought.

Because he was tugging down the scrap of white lace that was her knickers, and then they were gone too, and there was nothing at all between her and his merciless golden stare.

She was naked now. Naked in front of her husband.

He adjusted his hold on her again so she was lying back in his arms, her body stretched out, completely bare to his gaze. And she trembled slightly, waiting for the urge to run and hide, to cringe away.

But it didn't come. Instead she wanted to stretch out under his hot stare, to watch the flames in his eyes burn higher. Wanted to see how she affected him. Because she did, and it was obvious. The beautiful lines of his face were sharpening with hunger.

How strange... Though she was in the water, and completely naked, she felt more powerful than she had standing before him fully dressed. Like that day in his office, when she'd got an inkling of how much she affected him. Though that had only been a ghost of what she felt now.

Now her power was fully realised.

Brave in a way she hadn't been before, she lifted her hand and touched one carved cheek-bone, running her fingers along his smooth, warm skin.

Something ignited in his eyes and he made a growling sound deep in his throat. Then abruptly he turned, carrying her out of the water and to-wards the little cluster of tents pitched in the shadow of the trees.

He ducked inside the biggest one, and Char-lotte had an impression of a floor covered in silken rugs, with low couches and cushions set up in one corner, before Tariq threw her, still dripping wet, onto a huge bed with a carved wooden base. It was made up with fresh white cotton sheets and piled high with pillows, and it was incredibly comfortable. Not that she was particularly concerned with comfort right now.

He didn't follow her right away, his hands going to his own soaking wet wedding robes and stripping them off carelessly, leaving them in a heap on the floor. She found herself watching him, unable to look away.

She knew what he looked like naked because of the baths, and he was every bit as magnificent as she remembered. Yet this time, as he shoved down the loose trousers he'd been wearing, and with them his underwear, she was able to see what the water of the baths had been concealing.

Heat leapt inside her. Her face was burning… everything was burning.

He made no attempt to hide the long, hard length that curved up between his thighs, stepping naked and arrogant from his wet clothes. She couldn't stop looking at him.

He'd told her that it wasn't wrong to want him, that physical passion wasn't anything to be afraid of, but she couldn't help the apprehension that coiled inside her now. And it wasn't because she was afraid of him. She was afraid of herself, and of the hunger inside her getting deeper. Stronger.

After her parents' divorce intensity had always

scared her, so this was frightening. She wanted him so much. Part of her wished he'd push her back on the bed and take her the way she imagined kings took their brides. Hard and fast, with no mercy. Then she would have no choice but to give everything to him. No choice but to surrender to that hunger and not think about how to ignore it or force it away.

Not think about where that hunger might lead.

Except Tariq didn't make a move towards her. He stood there, staring at her, his demanding gaze hot on hers.

'Come to me,' he commanded.

Heat pulsed down her spine before spiralling into a tight knot down low between her thighs. She found herself obeying almost helplessly, pushing herself off the bed and walking the few steps that separated them. Her pulse was hammering in her ears as she came close, deafening her, and her mouth was bone-dry. She felt dizzy, but she didn't think it was the heat of the sun this time.

No, it was him.

Her husband.

He was so tall, towering over her, a wall of

heat, hard muscle and bronzed skin. And the expression on his face was ferocious.

'You want me,' he said.

It wasn't a question, but she answered all the same. 'Yes…' Her voice sounded hoarse and thick, the word unsteady.

'Say it,' he ordered, relentless.

Her heartbeat was racing, the strength of her own need building like a storm. He was going to demand an acknowledgement from her, that was obvious, which meant the time for pretending was over and she knew it. It would be pointless anyway—especially when he saw straight through her.

'I…want you,' she whispered.

His eyes gleamed, and his obvious pleasure made something hot glow inside her chest.

'Then go down on your knees, *ya amar*, and show me how much.'

Tariq knew he was indulging himself. That he didn't have to make his virgin wife go on her knees before him. But what she'd said to him out in the oasis had stuck in his head.

'Kind', she'd called him.

And so he'd stripped her bare, trying to

prove—to her, to himself—that he was nothing of the sort. Yet even then, naked and wet in his arms, she'd looked up at him as if she knew something about him that he didn't, lifting her hand to touch his cheek.

And perhaps she did know something he didn't. Because the second her cool fingers had touched him something had opened up inside him—a hunger he hadn't realised he felt. A hunger that had nothing to do with sexual desire. And he had known all at once that she was more dangerous than he could possibly have imagined.

No one had touched him like that since his mother had died. Not without any sexual intent, not casually or just because they'd wanted to. Not even the succession of nannies who'd brought him up had done so. They'd been given strict orders not to touch him or to comfort him—no reassurance or support had been allowed. Because he'd had to learn self-sufficiency, to find consolation in detachment and isolation, since that would be his life as king.

It had been a very hard lesson, but he'd learned it in the end. And it had taken Catherine to finally hammer it home. Since then he hadn't missed it—hadn't wanted the comfort of another person's touch. He'd had lovers to meet his physical needs and that was all he'd required.

Until Charlotte. Until her cool fingers had touched his cheek. Her touch delicate, tentative. Gentle.

He'd guarded himself against *her* vulnerability; he had just never dreamed she would discover something vulnerable in *him*.

What was clear was that he couldn't let that happen. He couldn't let her take that power from him. Which meant he had to show her where the power truly lay: with him.

She'd already given him the acknowledgement that she wanted him, and it clearly wasn't a stretch for her to obey him as she dropped to her knees on the soft rugs of the tent floor.

She was breathing very fast, the sound of it was audible in the tent, so he reached down and grasped her chin, tilting her head back so he could see her face, look into her eyes. They were very dark, the silver blue of a daytime sky turning to midnight. It was immensely satisfying to see how badly she wanted him.

'Open your mouth.' He pressed his thumb to the centre of her bottom lip for emphasis. 'Take me inside.'

'I… I haven't done this before.' Her cheeks were pink and she sounded breathless, a little uncertain. 'I'm not sure what to do.'

'That is why I will instruct you.' He stroked the softness of her lips, admiring her courage, because this time he couldn't see any apprehension in her at all. 'Do as you are told.'

She took a little breath, then opened her mouth obediently.

Ah, she made such a pretty picture, kneeling before him, naked and wet, her nipples pink and hard, her thighs spread, giving him a tantalising glimpse of the nest of blonde curls between them.

He was aching as he took himself in hand, guiding himself to her mouth. He gritted his teeth as she leaned forward, touching him with her tongue, tentative and hesitant. And then heat wrapped around him, slick warmth, as she took him into her mouth, and his heartbeat was as loud as a drum in his head, pleasure licking like a velvet whip up his spine.

He growled, unable to help himself, shoving his fingers in her hair and holding her, guiding her, as she began to suck him. She was inexpert and uncertain, but there was an eroticism to her inexperience that made pleasure burn like hot coals inside him. And knowing that he was the first man she'd ever done this to made it even more intense.

The first man. The *only* man.

His lips pulled back in a snarl as the thought hit him, and as her tongue curled around him it came to him all of a sudden that perhaps he'd made a mistake. Perhaps what had been intended to put her at a distance had only served to draw her closer. Because she had the power to undo him—he knew that now. With her hot mouth and her innocence, with her hesitant tongue and her cool fingers.

She could undo him completely right where he stood—and that was not what he'd intended at all.

Tariq tightened his grip, pulling her head away.

Her eyes widened in surprise. Her mouth was full and pink and slick from taking him.

'Did I—?' she began.

But he didn't let her finish, hauling her to her feet and kissing her hard and deep and territorial. She gave a little moan, shuddering in his hands, arching her body into his.

Ah, but he had to take control. He needed her

to be the one desperate for him, not the other way around. He couldn't allow her to get to him any more than she had already.

He picked her up, holding her warm body against him. Her skin was still cool and damp from the oasis, but now she was starting to warm up. Silky little woman. He was going to have to go slowly and carefully if he wanted this to last.

Crossing the few steps to the bed, he lowered her onto the mattress and followed, coming onto his hands and knees over her, watching the expressions across her face shift like the wind on the surface of a lake.

She was panting, her breasts rising and falling fast, her pretty nipples were tight and the flush in her cheeks had spread down her neck and over her chest. Her thighs had fallen open, baring her sex to his gaze: slick pink skin and a cluster of silver-blonde curls.

Beautiful. Delicate.

Yours.

He looked into her eyes, watching her as he lifted a hand and brushed her throat with his fingertips, then ran them lightly down the centre of her body, stroking her satiny skin. She shuddered, goosebumps rising in the wake of his touch, her breasts and stomach quivering. He didn't stop, and he didn't look away as his fingers brushed the soft curls between her thighs and then the slick, hot folds beneath them.

She gasped, her hips rising to his hand, her eyes going wide. Her pleasure was obvious. The musky, sweet scent of her arousal was like a drug, turning his hunger sharp as knife. But it wasn't his desire he wanted to sharpen. It was hers. So he parted her gently with his fingers, finding the hard bud that would give her the most pleasure and teasing it lightly. She groaned and jerked, panting.

'Arms above your head,' he ordered softly. 'And do not take them down until I say.'

'T-Tariq, I don't know if I—'

'Trust me, *ya amar.*'

She took another shuddering breath, then slowly raised her arms and let them rest on the pillows behind her head. Her gaze was on his, as if he was the centre of the entire universe, and he liked that. Liked the way she trusted him. Liked it far, far too much.

'Yes,' he murmured, stroking and teasing her. 'Look at me. Keep looking at me.'

She shook, gasping as he slid his fingers over

her slickness, her hips lifting restlessly. 'Tariq...' Her voice was thick and desperate. 'Oh... I can't... This— This is...'

He lowered his head and stopped her words with his mouth, kissing her hard and deep. She groaned, letting him in. The taste of her was the same as it had been in the baths, achingly sweet, and it made him feel wild, made his restraint feel thin and tenuous.

But he was used to testing himself, so he kissed her harder, letting his fingers find the slick entrance to her body and circling it, tantalising her, before gradually easing inside. She was tight, her body clamping down on his fingers, and the hot, wet heat of her pulled hard on the leash he'd placed on his control.

She arched beneath him, moaning, her hands gripping onto the pillows above her head and twisting. He took his mouth from hers and kissed down the delicate arch of her neck, tasting the salt in the hollow of her throat, and then further, between her breasts. He covered one nipple with his lips and sucked, teasing it with his tongue as he stroked his fingers in and out of her.

She called his name, gasping. Her eyes were

closed, her head thrown back, her silver hair sticking to her forehead and neck.

Beautiful. Desperate. His.

He moved his mouth to her other breast and at the same time pressed his thumb down on that small bud between her thighs, sliding his fingers deep. She cried out, her body stiffening as the climax washed over her.

Her taste was in his mouth and her scent was all around, the sound of her pleasure loud in his ears.

And his control hung by a thread.

He could not wait any longer.

Pulling his fingers from her body, he knelt between her thighs and slid his hands beneath the shapely curve of her bottom, lifting her, fitting himself to the entrance of her body.

He put one hand down on the pillow beside her head and leaned over her, looking down into her eyes.

Then he thrust deep and hard inside her.

CHAPTER NINE

CHARLOTTE GASPED, ARCHING against the deep, firm, relentless push of Tariq inside her. The sensitive tissues of her sex stretched around him, taking him. Then she cried out, shuddering. Because it was overwhelming and strange and yet somehow so good she didn't have words for it.

He was stretched out above her, his golden eyes burning down into hers, and for a moment an intense sense of wonder was all there was. Her friends, whenever they'd talked about sex, had mentioned that the first time could be painful, but that it was in the end very pleasurable. But they'd never mentioned this sense of...closeness. Of connection. The intense intimacy of having another person inside you.

She didn't feel pain right now, only that sense of connection blazing through her and into him, joining them together in a way that wasn't possible at any other time, in any other way.

It wasn't anything like she'd expected. She'd

had a glimpse of it as she'd knelt at his feet, taking him into her mouth, the taste of him rich and salty on her tongue. His expression had been so fierce, and she'd loved the pleasure she'd seen flare in the golden depths of his gaze. But then he'd pulled away, and she'd thought that perhaps she'd done something wrong—until he'd taken her on the bed and put his hands on her. And then she hadn't thought at all, completely lost as he'd touched her…made the world explode behind her eyes.

But this was different—this was mutual. Giving to each other.

He held her gaze—held it so completely that it felt as if he was touching her both inside and out—and then he shifted, gripping her wrists and holding them down on the pillows above her, adjusting himself so he could push even deeper.

She couldn't speak—didn't have the breath… didn't have the words either. All she could do was look up at him in amazement that this was happening between them, that it could feel like this.

And it wasn't frightening. It wasn't frightening in any way.

Strange and a little uncomfortable, yes, but not scary.

He began to move, drawing his hips back and then pushing in again, the slide of him inside her making her gasp. She could feel her body adjustiing to him, and soon it wasn't uncomfortable or strange as pleasure began to radiate, curling through her. She began to move with him, responding to an instinct that felt as if it had always been there, and it made the light in his eyes blaze brighter.

He murmured something in his beautiful language, the liquid whisper of sound almost a caress in itself. She wanted to touch him, run her hands all over him, feel the hard strength of his muscles and taste his skin, but the way he was holding her down and the movement of him inside her made that impossible.

She moaned as the pleasure gathered strength, urging him to move faster, and he did, going deeper, harder, and it was so good. So very, *very* good that even the thought of how afraid she'd been of this was impossible to imagine.

This wasn't shouting or bitterness. This wasn't anger or pain. This was wonder and joy and connection.

Careful. Be careful.

But she couldn't think about that now. She couldn't think at all as pleasure spiralled higher and higher, gathering inside her, tighter and tighter.

She wound her legs around Tariq's lean hips and moved with him, becoming demanding, getting desperate, calling his name and not caring, giving herself up to the relentless build of sensation.

And then he shifted, lifting one hand from her wrist and slipping it down between her legs, touching her where all the pleasure seemed to centre at the same time as he thrust one last time, deep and hard. And the world exploded into flames around her, making her scream his name as the molten gold of his eyes seemed to consume her whole.

She lost herself after that, dimly aware of him suddenly moving hard and fast, and then the stiffening of his body and the sound of her name as he found his own pleasure.

Then he was on top of her, heavy as a mountain falling, his breath hot in her ear, and the heat of his body was burning her alive. He remained like that for a couple of breathless seconds and she didn't mind at all. His weight and the hard muscle against her was making her feel safe. Bringing her back to earth and anchoring her.

Then his arms came around her and she was held fast against him as he turned over onto his back, taking her with him so she was at last resting on his broad chest. And they remained like that for long minutes, not speaking, with the silence of the desert filtering through the thin tent walls.

'Did I hurt you?' he asked after a long moment, his fingers trailing in a long caress down her back.

His chest was so warm, his skin so smooth, with a light prickle of hair, and he smelled salty and musky and absolutely delicious. She couldn't stop herself from pressing her mouth to his skin.

'No, not at all.' She kissed him again, then glanced up, smiling a little shyly. 'It was amazing.'

He didn't smile back, the set of his mouth grim. Yet she could see the after-effects of pleasure glowing like hot coals in his eyes. Something tight collected inside her. Had he not enjoyed it? It had seemed as if he had, and yet his expression said the opposite.

'It wasn't amazing?' She swallowed, searching his face. 'I tried not to disappoint—'

She broke off as his fingers tangled abruptly in her hair and he lowered his head for a hard kiss, his mouth ravaging hers with an intensity that left her breathless.

'You did not disappoint,' he growled, releasing her.

Panting slightly, she stared at him, bewildered. 'Then why are you looking like you'd never had a worse experience in your life?'

His eyes glittered, the expression in them still impossible to read. 'You are dangerous, *ya amar.* Do you know that?'

'Dangerous?' she repeated blankly, not understanding. 'How am I dangerous?'

'A king is supposed to be isolated. He should remain detached or else face having his judgement impaired.' He untangled his fingers from her hair, and one thumb stroked the back of her neck in an absent movement, as if he couldn't help himself. 'I cannot risk my judgement being impaired.'

She leaned back into his hand, loving his caress, yet remaining puzzled by his words. 'What's that got to do with me being dangerous?'

'You are a threat to my detachment.' His voice had got lower, rougher, and the fierce glow in his eyes was burning bright. 'And to my judgement. So you need to understand that this marriage will be a physical one only. Is that clear?'

Something in her gut twisted, as if in distress. Which was strange, because she hadn't expected anything from this marriage at all. But this didn't sound bad. In fact, if sex was like that every time, then there didn't appear to be a down side. It was good, even. If it was only sex, then there was no risk of feelings entering into the mix— no risk of it turning poisonous like her parents' marriage.

'Yes,' she said, folding her hands on his chest and resting her chin on them. 'I understand.'

'Good.'

The starkly beautiful lines of his face relaxed and he ran the backs of his fingers down her cheek in a light caress that made goosebumps erupt everywhere.

'Now, tell me why such a passionate woman has remained a virgin so long.'

She let out a long breath. It didn't feel so bad to be telling him—not here, not with his big muscular body spread out beneath hers.

'I told you that my parents had a very bitter divorce? Well, their relationship was…uh…volatile, to say the least. Lots of shouting at each other. Lots of screaming. Especially towards the end.' She rubbed her thumb across his skin, tracing a little circle. 'I thought if that was what a relationship was all about, then I didn't want anything to do with one.'

'Understandable. You can have sex without a relationship, however.'

'I know.' She lifted a shoulder. 'I just never met anyone I wanted enough.'

His gaze was very focused, very intense. 'Never met anyone you let yourself want, you mean.'

Charlotte sighed. 'I suppose you're right. I didn't want to risk getting involved with anyone, considering how bad it had been with Mum and Dad. And it's probably a good thing—especially now.'

'Why especially now?'

She could feel her cheeks redden. Did she really have to explain it to him? Surely he would know?

'Well, sex is pretty amazing, isn't it? I mean, I

don't know how you could experience that and not get involved with someone.'

Something flickered in his eyes, and again she couldn't read it.

'You say that like it is always that way. It is not, Charlotte.'

She waited for him to elaborate, but he didn't. And suddenly she understood. What she had felt between them—that sense of connection—he must have felt too. And it wasn't usual.

That's why you're dangerous to him. And that's why he is dangerous to you too.

'Oh…' she said faintly, the tangle of emotions in her gut knotting tighter. 'I didn't know.'

'Of course you did not.' His expression didn't change, his focus remaining on her. 'But it is a good thing that you do now. And it is also a good thing for us that we have such physical chemistry.'

She could hear what he didn't say.

Because there will be no one else for either of us.

Knowing that didn't upset her—not as she'd thought it might. The fact was that she didn't want anyone else. Even the thought of having another man touch her, be inside her the way Tariq had been, made her feel cold.

But that connection you felt with him will only ever be in bed.

Of course it would. That was fine, though. She didn't need to have that sense of connection anywhere else.

She met his gaze and smiled. She ignored the small kernel of ice that sat in the pit of her stomach. 'You didn't mind that I was inexperienced?' she asked.

'No, *ya amar.* Not in the slightest.'

'Why do you call me that? I'm not your "most beautiful".'

'Yes, you are,' he disagreed. 'Now you are my wife you will always be my most beautiful. And because your hair is silver, and you are so pale, you are like the moon, Charlotte.'

The words made something warm glow in the centre of her chest. She'd never been given an endearment like that before. She'd never been given an endearment at all, and she liked it. Especially the idea of being his moon when he was the sun.

'What about you?' She stared up at him, suddenly curious. 'What were your parents like?'

A shadow crossed his face, gone so quickly

that if she hadn't been looking she might not have seen it at all.

'My mother died when I was very young, so I did not know her. And my father was…very strict.'

Her curiosity tightened at this odd hesitation, which seemed uncharacteristic for him. 'Oh? How so?'

But he only shook his head, reaching for her again. 'Not now.' His hand cupped the back of her head and exerted pressure, urging her towards him. 'Now I need to make certain that my people get the heir I promised them.'

And then her mouth was on his and there was no more talking.

He kept her in the tent for a few more hours after that, making her desperate for him over and over, making her forget about everything but her frantic need to have him inside her.

And after that, when twilight had begun to fall, he arranged her outside on the divan beneath the palms, and made her sit there with a glass of wine while he prepared the food that had been delivered by palace staff.

Solar-powered lighting strung around the palms gave the oasis a soft illumination and later, after they'd eaten a delicious meal and the darkness had closed in, Tariq lit a fire with capable hands, then wrapped her in a blanket that he'd brought from the tent, making her lean back in his arms as they talked.

He was not forthcoming about his family, but he was passionate about his people and his country, talking at length about his plans to keep Ashkaraz thriving. There was no doubting his conviction or his vision, and his drive to protect his people was incredibly attractive.

He was incredibly attractive full stop.

'Why do you keep the borders closed?' she asked after a small lull in the conversation, with her hands wrapped around a mug of the most delicious hot chocolate she'd ever tasted. 'And why do you give the outside world the impression of being a narrow and vicious ruler?'

He'd risen to put more wood on the fire, wearing only a pair of loose black trousers. The flames played over his impressive chest, making her fingers itch to touch him again, but the answer to this was important. Too important to be distracted from.

Crouching, he added another stick to the flames from the pile beside him. Firelight limned the fierce planes and angles of his face in gold, making him look like a hero of old, bringing fire from the gods for the good of mankind.

'You have not read our history, then?' he asked, not looking up from what he was doing. 'That is what you were told to do.'

She flushed. 'I know—and I did. But I started way back, when Ashkaraz first became Ashkaraz. I haven't got to any recent history yet.'

'All you need to know will be in the books.'

There was a note of warning in his tone, an edge that made her gaze narrow. 'You don't want to tell me yourself?'

'No.' The word was flat and hard. The command of a king.

Puzzled, Charlotte gazed at him. Recent history seemed a strange thing to be recalcitrant about, but she was reluctant to push it since they'd reached a pleasant equilibrium. Perhaps she should leave it. She was enjoying sitting out here with him, watching him do things for her and talking with him about all kinds of trivialities. He had a dry sense of humour that appealed to her, and he knew far more about the outside world and its politics than she'd thought he would.

Pushing him would definitely make things tense, and she did hate that. Then again, he'd been constantly pushing her since she'd arrived in Ashkaraz, and much to her own surprise she hadn't backed down. So why should she now? He'd made her reveal her father's disappointment in her—why shouldn't he give a little in return?

Why should you care?

Not wanting that particular thought, Charlotte shoved it away.

'Why not?' she asked carefully. 'If I'm going to find out sooner or later, I'd much rather hear it from you first.'

The fire glowed in the darkness, radiating heat, casting a warm light over Charlotte, wrapped in a blanket. Her hair lay loose over her bare shoulders and he was very aware that she hadn't bothered to dress. That she was naked underneath that blanket.

It would be easy to go over to her, pull away the blanket and lay her down before the fire. Make her scream his name to the stars above their heads the way he had in the tent earlier. But there was a danger in that too—as he'd discovered the minute he'd pushed inside her. When he'd looked down into her eyes and read the wonder and amazement in them as she'd looked back at him. Staring at him as if he'd given her all the secrets of the universe.

'Dangerous' he'd called her, and she was.

But at least in bed he could keep it all about physical pleasure. Out here by the fire, with her lovely face lit by the flames, her gaze level and very direct, there were no such comforting lies.

Why are you so reluctant to tell her the truth? Why does it matter?

He didn't know. What he did know, however, was that he could not allow his reluctance to win. He had to be very careful with her around, to ensure his detachment was solid—especially considering how she threatened it.

Which meant, of course, that he had to tell her.

Ignoring the strange reluctance that pulled at him, Tariq straightened up. 'What is there to say? My father had an American lover whose family was very keen on knowing the secret of our wealth, so she tried hard to get that secret from him. But he would not tell her.'

He looked at Charlotte over the flames.

'So she turned her sights on me. I was seventeen and…angry with my father for various reasons. So I let her seduce me. And when she asked where our country got its wealth from I told her about the oil reserves in the north.'

Charlotte frowned. 'You meant to tell her?'

'I was in love with her.'

You were not. You told her because you wanted to punish your father.

The thought was a whisper in his head, highlighting the lie he'd just told Charlotte. The lie he'd always told himself. But it wasn't really a lie, was it?

His father had denied him something he'd wanted passionately and desperately and he'd been *so* angry. So he'd allowed Catherine to seduce him. Allowed her to get under his skin. Allowed himself to give away his country's secrets. Because he could blame it all on love.

Except it hadn't been love. It had been selfishness—his own needs put before his country's.

Sympathy glowed in Charlotte's eyes, and an understanding he didn't deserve.

'Oh, Tariq,' she murmured. 'I'm so sorry.'

'What are you sorry for?' he said brusquely. 'It is not your fault.'

'No, but you think it's yours, don't you?'

'It *is* mine.' More than she knew.

'You were only seventeen.'

'Old enough to know better.'

He knew he sounded cold, but he couldn't afford to make it any different. Nor could he afford to lean into that sympathy and understanding he saw in her face.

'I sold my country out for love.' Which was not entirely untrue. 'It will not happen again.'

The flames played over her pretty face, lighting her pale with a golden glow, and the searching way she was looking at him made him want to push her back on the sand and take her hard, to distract her.

'That's not all there is, though, is it?' she said quietly. 'There's more to the story.'

How she knew that, he wasn't quite sure. But it wasn't anything he'd share with her. She didn't need to know the true extent of his pettiness.

Why should it matter what she thinks anyway?

He ignored the thought. 'There is nothing that you cannot find out from the books in the library,' he said, and stepped around the fire, coming over to where she sat, her hands still wrapped around the mug of hot chocolate he'd made for her.

She tilted her head back, looking up at him. 'Why won't you tell me?'

The question was so simple, so honest and open. And something within him wanted to respond. To tell her the truth about the aching loneliness of his childhood. The need he'd had for someone—anyone—and how that had always been denied him. Until one day he'd broken.

You cannot tell her. A king must be self-sufficient. Detached. Alone.

He knew it—had learned his lesson and learned it well. Catherine had been his teacher in that, even though she hadn't realised it herself. She'd given him what his father had never allowed: someone to talk to, confide in. And he *had* confided in her, and part of him had known his error even as he'd told her about the oil. Known and yet he'd done it anyway. Because he had been angry.

Because you couldn't bear to be lonely and you hated your father for the way he kept you isolated. You were a selfish boy and you nearly destroyed your country because of it.

Charlotte frowned, and he had the strange impression that she could read every thought in his head, because she put her mug down in the sand and rose to her feet, her blanket caught awkwardly around her. She stepped forward and put her arms around him, leaning her head on his chest.

There was nothing sexual in it. It was merely a hug.

He'd never been hugged before. Not by his father, nor by the nannies who'd brought him up. So the feel of Charlotte's arms around him shocked him. Made him freeze in place. He felt as if there was an animal inside him, struggling to get free of a cage, and as if any move he made would spring the cage door wide open.

He didn't know what would happen if that animal got free.

You know what happens.

Yes, he did. Disaster.

His instinct was urging him to shove her away, but that would hurt her, and for some reason the thought of hurting her caused him actual pain. So he was forced to stand there and endure the hug she was giving him, even though he didn't want it.

'I'm sorry,' she said, her voice muffled against his chest. 'You don't have to tell me if it's painful.'

He had no idea how he'd given himself away. And no idea of what to say to her now either.

Earlier that day she'd told him about the way her father had treated her and he'd seen how painful that had been for her. How her parents' bad marriage had made her afraid of getting involved with anyone.

He'd thought initially that was a good thing, that her fear would prevent her from getting too close. But the way she was holding him now made it clear that it wasn't as simple as that.

She wasn't afraid to ask him about the things he didn't want to talk about. Or to offer him comfort. She wasn't afraid to show him she cared. And she wasn't thinking of herself or her fear right now. She was only thinking of him.

His heart ached, raw and painful in his chest.

He wanted to tell her his secrets. Wanted to share those hours he'd spent in the desert at a young age, taken out and left there alone so he could develop self-reliance. Those days of silence in the palace, when he had been forbidden company so he could learn how to deal with loneliness. Days of not seeing anyone. Not speaking to anyone.

Sometimes he would hear laughter, the shouts of children in the courtyards outside, and he'd wanted so much to go out and play. But he had never been allowed.

Alone, his father had told him. *A king always stands alone. Because he is stronger that way.*

She was warm against him, all soft, silky bare skin and the sweet scent of her body.

Telling her the truth only means something if you let it.

And it didn't have to, did it? After all, it had happened a very long time ago. He was making amends for his mistake now. He wouldn't let it rule him. So what did it matter if she knew about what he'd done? It might even be a lesson to her to keep her distance. He'd told her back in the tent that they would never have a normal marriage, but it wouldn't hurt to drive that message home.

Tariq could feel his body already responding to her nearness, but all he did was raise his hands and gently put her from him. He would not make this about sex now. Not yet, at least.

She frowned and opened her mouth, but he laid a finger on her soft lips, silencing her.

'I was not entirely truthful,' he said quietly. 'I

did love Catherine. But…that was not the reason I told her about my country's wealth.'

Puzzlement flickered over Charlotte's features. 'Oh?'

'My father had…set ideas on how a ruler should be brought up. He believed that a king must always stand apart, and that is how he raised me. Always apart. I was not allowed friends, or companions of any kind, and no comfort from any of the nannies who looked after me. A king has to be used to loneliness, so he made sure I got used to it from a very early age.'

Charlotte stared at him in obvious shock. 'No friends? None?'

'No.' He refused to allow the expression on her face to affect him. 'It was not so bad as a child. But as I got older I found it more…difficult. My father had always stressed the importance of a good education, so I thought I could at least get a taste of what life would be like if I was not a king and go to university. I applied to Oxford, unbeknownst to my father, and was accepted. But…'

He'd thought his anger long since blunted by now, but it wasn't. Even after so many years he could still feel its sharp edge. It deepened his voice to a growl.

'My father would not let me go. I argued with him, shouted at him, but he would not be moved. He even put guards on my door in case I tried to sneak away.' Tariq looked down into Charlotte's pale face. 'I was so angry. So very, *very* angry. And when one night I saw Catherine, weeping beside a fountain in the gardens, I knew I'd found an opportunity to get back at him. She wanted me and I let her seduce me. And when she asked me about Ashkaraz's secret, I told her.'

'Oh, Tariq…' There was nothing but sympathy in Charlotte's expression.

'I told her because I was angry,' he went on, so she fully understood. 'Because I was petty. Because I was selfish. I told her because I had not learned the lessons my father had tried to teach me about detachment. About not letting my emotions control me or affect my judgement. I did what a ruler is never supposed to do, and that is to put his own feelings before his country.'

There was no judgement in Charlotte's eyes, only distress. She reached out and put a hand on his chest.

'Of course you were angry. You wanted some time to be a normal teenager.'

But he didn't want her pain on his behalf. Didn't want her sympathy. Not when he didn't deserve any of it.

'That is no excuse. I should have listened to what he was trying to teach me, yet I did not. I was just a spoiled boy who wanted something his father would not give him.'

'No!' Charlotte shot back, suddenly fierce. 'You weren't spoiled, Tariq. You were lonely. Terribly, desperately lonely.'

'I betrayed my country, Charlotte.' He made it explicit, because it was clear that she did *not* understand. 'Out of nothing more than selfishness. There can be no excuses for that. No forgiveness. There is only atonement and my dedication to make sure it does not happen again.'

She closed her mouth, but the distress in her eyes lingered and he didn't like it, didn't want her to feel it—because it made that animal inside him claw at the cage, wound the tension in his shoulders even tighter. Made him want to take her in his arms and hold her, take the distress away.

But he couldn't allow himself that. And there

was one way he could get rid of that look in her eyes. One way to ease her distress.

Tariq put his palm over hers on his chest, then lifted his other hand, tugging the blanket from around her. She made no move to grab it, standing there warm and naked in the firelight.

'Tariq…' she whispered.

But whatever else she'd been going to say was lost as he reached for her, gathering her up in his arms. And then he stopped her mouth entirely with his, and made them both forget about history and pain and loneliness.

At least for a little while.

CHAPTER TEN

CHARLOTTE SAT IN the palace library on one of
the low couches near the window, with the sound
of the fountain drifting in from the garden outside. The early-evening air was warm and full of
the smell of flowers, and she could hear a couple
of the gardeners out amongst the rose bushes,
talking in low voices.

Her Arabic wasn't good enough yet for her
to be able to tell what they were talking about,
but she recognised the odd word here and there.
Something about football.

It reminded her of her flatmates in England
and made her smile—at least until a wave of
homesickness hit her. Strange to feel that way
about a place where she hadn't much enjoyed living anyway, but she did. And it didn't help that
she'd spent the last couple of weeks since getting
back from the oasis on her own. Tariq had disappeared into the endless meetings and official

business that took up a lot of his time, and she barely saw him at all during the day.

It wasn't as if she'd been completely left to her own devices, though. She had her own royal duties as sheikha, and that was taking some getting used to, plus she had a lot of study to do in order to get up to speed on the customs and history of Ashkaraz, as well as more language and protocol classes.

She might have been fascinated by all this, and certainly she would have enjoyed it a lot more, if her head hadn't been quite so full of her husband.

Ever since those three days at the oasis he was all she could think about. What he'd told her about his childhood had shocked her. To be kept alone and apart from everyone, denied friendship and even simple human comfort, must have been horrific.

It made her wonder about the ferocity that burned in his eyes and the sense of volcanic emotions simmering just below the surface, kept tightly leashed and locked down. How would such loneliness have affected such a passionate man?

Well, she didn't need to wonder. He'd told her. He'd been broken and the consequences had been awful. And so terribly unfair. Because it wasn't his fault he'd been pushed to breaking point.

Her throat tightened, her eyes prickling with unexpected tears. That night at the oasis he'd told her about it so flatly, so emotionlessly, and yet she'd seen the rage that burned bright in his eyes. Rage that was still there even all these years later. And not only that, it seemed to her that he was still punishing himself for that youthful mistake, denying himself the emotional outlet that he so clearly needed.

Why do you care so much about this?

Charlotte pushed the book she'd been reading off her lap and stood, pacing over to the windows and back to the couch again, restless.

She cared because she knew what it was like to be pushed into making a mistake that you wished you could take back. And she cared because he was her husband. Because he was a kind man, no matter that he said he wasn't, and he believed in what he was doing. Because he was passionate.

Pacing back to the windows, Charlotte looked out sightlessly at the rose bushes and the fountains, her heart beating far too fast for comfort. She couldn't stop thinking about him. Couldn't stop thinking about those three days she'd spent with him.

It hadn't been the same after that first night, though the sex had been incendiary. It hadn't been the same since they'd returned to the palace either, with them seeing each other only when Tariq needed her physically. Their bed the only place where it felt as if they communicated fully with each other. Where they were joined and words weren't needed…where their pasts were irrelevant.

What would it be like if they had that feeling outside the bedroom too?

Ah, but there was no point thinking about that. It was impossible. He'd told her their marriage would only be a physical one, that he couldn't give her any kind of emotional connection. She'd thought she'd have no problem with that, but maybe she did.

You never wanted a marriage like your parents', but what if that's how yours ends up?

A cold thread wound through her, making her fingers feel icy. That could happen, couldn't it? Tariq might strive for detachment, but she would always be able to sense the hidden currents that shifted beneath his hard, merciless surface. She could feel his anger and his passion, see it in his eyes, sense it burning him alive.

And then it would be like it had been at home, with her parents' bitterness and animosity battering her, surrounding her. With her wanting to take away their anger and pain but not knowing how. Until the day she'd broken away and run from it all, and made everything ten thousand times worse.

You can't run away now, though.

No, she couldn't. She was married to a king and she couldn't leave even if she'd wanted to. But she didn't want to. She wanted to stay, to help him, to turn her marriage into something good for both of them.

Except what could she do when he was determined to stay detached?

Carefully, she went over what he'd told her out at the oasis again—about the dreadful childhood he'd had, with no one and nothing to ease his loneliness.

Lonely, that was what he was. So maybe all he needed was a friend. Someone to talk to, to confide in. Someone who wouldn't make any emotional demands on him.

She could do that, couldn't she?

She could be his friend?

'I have been looking for you.'

There was no mistaking the dark, deep voice that echoed through the room, making her jump.

She turned, looking towards the double doors that were standing open. Tariq's tall, muscled frame was filling the doorway. His hot golden stare found hers and her mouth dried, her cheeks heating.

She knew that look. He had it when he wanted her. And he often did during the day, coming to find her wherever she was and taking her by the hand, leading her to his rooms or to somewhere secluded, where he would strip her bare and take her, with that familiar ferocity molten in his eyes.

He didn't speak afterwards, just left her burned to ashes where she stood while he turned away and went back to doing whatever it was he'd been doing before he'd come to find her, apparently satisfied.

She had the sense that he wanted something from her in those moments, that it wasn't simply sex, but she never knew what it was.

Perhaps she might have an answer to that now.

He was in dark charcoal suit trousers and one of his exquisitely cut business shirts, this one in dark blue, making his bronze skin seem richer and highlighting the gold of his eyes. She was struck, as she always was, by the raw, stark beauty of him. By how amazing it was that a man like this was hers.

He is not yours, though. And he never will be. Just as you will never be his.

The sliver of glass sitting inside her twisted— a sharp, unexpected pain that seemed to radiate out from the centre of her chest.

Which was ridiculous. She'd never thought he would be hers and she'd never wanted him to be. So where this pain was coming from she had no idea, and it was best she simply ignored it.

He turned and locked the doors, then turned back, his stare becoming even hotter. 'Come here,' he ordered darkly.

She could feel her own need start to rise, ignited by the way he looked at her. It didn't take much to set her burning these days—not when he was around. But she couldn't let it get to her, not right now. She needed to say something first.

'Wait.' She took a steadying breath. 'I have something to say.'

His gaze narrowed. 'What?'

Okay, good. He was prepared to listen. 'I've

been thinking about what you said at the oasis. About your childhood.'

His inky brows pulled down in a scowl. 'That has nothing to do with you.'

'Yes, it does. You're my husband. You told me once that everything about me is your business, which also must mean that everything about you is mine.'

A certain kind of energy was gathering about him now, dark and electric and absolutely mesmerising. His golden stare held her fast, frozen where she stood, and the warning glitter in it made it obvious that he didn't like what she'd said.

But that was too bad. She hadn't let herself be intimidated by him since she'd arrived here and she wasn't about to start.

'I do not want to hear about this now,' Tariq growled, advancing on her. 'I have other needs first.'

But she knew what those needs were, and she had a suspicion that they weren't only to do with sex. That it was the forbidden connection he came in search of whenever he was in this mood. He would accept it if she offered it without strings. Without any need for him to return it.

'Or we could sit and talk.' She lifted her chin, looking him in the eye. 'Conversation, Tariq. You remember how to do that?'

He didn't stop, his lean-hipped hunter's stride closing the distance between them, his tiger's gaze on hers. 'I do not want to talk.'

She didn't have any time to evade him. One minute he was nowhere near her, the next he was gripping her hips and pulling her close.

She flung up her hands, pressing her palms against his hard chest, holding him away. 'I'm not trying to take anything from you or make you give me something in return,' she said, trying to master her own helpless physical response to him. 'I'm not going to demand anything from you. Just… If you need a friend, I can be one for you.'

He went very still, staring down at her, his eyes glittering. 'A friend?' He said the word as if he had no idea what it meant. 'Why would I need a friend?'

'Everyone does.' His chest was hot beneath her palms, his muscles like iron, stiff with tension. 'Even kings.'

'You are mistaken.' His fingers tightened on her. 'I have no need of a friend. Ever.'

But she could see behind the desire in his eyes and she knew what drove him. Because she felt it in herself. He wanted a connection just as badly as she did.

'How would you know?' she asked softly. 'When you've never had one?'

He made a deep, dismissive sound, pulling her closer, fitting her hips against his so she could feel the hard, demanding length of him through the silk of her robes.

'I have Faisal. And I have other advisors.'

Her heart clenched tight. Was that what he truly thought friends were? His royal advisors? An old family servant? But of course he would. He had no other reference, did he?

'They're not friends, Tariq.' She pressed her fingertips to the warm cotton of his shirt. 'They are employees. And that's not the same thing.'

He ignored her, taking her mouth in a hot, hard kiss that left her breathless and unsteady on her feet.

'You should sit down,' he growled. 'And stop talking.'

The kiss left her lips tingling, with the dark, rich taste of him on her tongue, and it would have been easy to let him keep going. To stop pushing him, to let him do what he wanted and make her mindless with pleasure right here in the library.

But that, in essence, would be running away again. That would be hiding under the table the way she'd used to do, or running into the woods. Curling around her pain like a wounded animal and keeping it inside, not letting it leak into the atmosphere and make everything worse.

Yet running hadn't solved anything. It had only caused her even more pain. She couldn't do that again. She had to make a stand.

Her hand slid from his chest and up, to cup his strong, beautiful face. 'You do know what a friend is, don't you?'

The gold of his eyes was like a sword spearing through her, full of sharp edges. 'Of course I do not,' he snapped. 'As you said before, I have never had one.' He pulled away from her suddenly and gestured to the low couch nearby. 'Sit down, Charlotte.'

Another order. And calling her 'Charlotte' meant he was displeased with her.

She studied the look on his face. He was angry, that was clear, and he didn't want her pushing him. Didn't want her reminding him of the past that still so obviously hurt him and the mistake he'd made because he was human, because he'd been a boy who'd desperately wanted someone.

She could show him that, couldn't she? She could show him what it was like to have someone. A friend and a lover. A wife. A support. It would mean opening herself up and not demanding anything from him. But that was what you had to do when you wanted to tame a beast, wasn't it?

Slowly and carefully you fed it your heart.

'Charlotte,' he repeated, low and dark. 'I gave you a command.'

His eyes glittered like golden flames burning behind glass and she was reminded of what she'd thought weeks ago: this man was a volcano. Harsh and cold on the outside, while underneath he seethed, molten with rage and passion, burning up inside because all those emotions had nowhere to go.

Well, maybe she would give them an outlet. That was what a friend would do.

'Your father was wrong, by the way,' Charlotte said steadily, moving over to the couch Tariq had indicated. 'He shouldn't have brought you up the way he did.'

She sat down, arranging her robes around her

and folding her hands in her lap. Then she looked up at him.

'No one can live in a vacuum, let alone a child. They'd suffocate.'

His face was impassive as he moved to where she sat, standing in front of her, hard and cold as granite. Yet the heat in his eyes was as unyielding and merciless as the desert sun.

'This conversation, wife, is over.' His voice was rough and hot, full of lava and gravel. 'Spread your legs for me.'

Tariq's heart was beating far too fast, and it felt as if the hungry animal in his chest, the one he kept caged and leashed, was sinking its claws into him once again. If he wasn't careful it would claw him to pieces entirely—and who knew what would happen then?

He remembered the disgust in his father's eyes as he'd looked at Tariq from across his desk...

'You are a disgrace,' Ishak had said angrily over the constant ringing of the phone, with the consequences of Tariq's betrayal already reverberating through Ashkaraz. *'After everything I have taught you, you have learned nothing.'* His father's expression had twisted. *'You are unwor-*

thy, Tariq. Unworthy of being my heir. Unworthy of being my son.'

The memory shuddered through him and he shoved it aside, concentrating instead on the woman sitting calmly on the couch in front of him, her blue gaze steady on his.

His chest ached, and a strange and molten anger was seething inside him. He didn't know what she was talking about. A friend? That was nonsense. What did he need a friend for? He'd never had one, it was true, but then, he'd never needed one.

He didn't need anyone.

A lie. You need her.

But only for sex. In fact, since coming back from the oasis it seemed as if sex with his wife was all he thought about. He couldn't concentrate on his duties, on the work he needed to do. Instead he found himself stalking the corridors of the palace in search of her, hard and aching. She would always give him what he wanted. And yet afterwards, when he should have been well sated, all he felt was hollow. Empty. Like Tantalus, for ever drinking and for ever thirsty.

It was inexplicable.

He felt it now as he looked down at her, sitting

on that couch in a spread of sky-blue silk. An aching emptiness. A hunger. A thirst.

She was wrong about suffocating in a vacuum. You'd only suffocate if you needed air to breathe, and he didn't. He'd trained himself to live without it. In fact, he'd prove it to her.

'You heard what I said.' His voice was too low and too rough. 'Do as you are told.'

She didn't protest, spreading her knees, her blue eyes full of the same understanding he'd seen in the firelight that night at the oasis.

'Did you know that one night I ran away from home?' she said quietly. 'My parents had been arguing more than usual and I couldn't stand it. I stayed out all night and they ended up calling the police.'

Tariq ignored her, dropping to his knees in front of her. He put his hands on her thighs and pushed them apart, spreading her wider.

'They searched for hours,' Charlotte went on. 'I heard them calling my name but I didn't answer. I didn't want to go back home and listen to all that shouting. They found me, though, and dragged me back.'

Why was she telling him this? He didn't want to hear it. He wanted to hear nothing but her gasps of pleasure and her sighs. The way she called his name just as she was about to come.

He took the hem of her robes in his fists.

'My parents were so angry. And my mother decided that I was too much trouble to fight over, so she let Dad have custody of me.' Her voice wavered slightly. 'Even though he didn't really want me.'

The material was soft in his hands, the scent of her body sweet. His hunger was pulsing in time with his heartbeat and he didn't know why he'd stopped. Didn't understand why that tremble in her voice had made his chest ache.

'I know you may not want me either,' she continued. 'Not for anything more than sex. But if you need someone to talk to or just…be with, I will be that person for you.'

The words hurt—sticking inside him like thorns, piercing him right through. Which was ridiculous.

He didn't want someone to talk to or 'be with'—whatever that meant. He had Faisal. He had his council. And as for her—well, he needed her for one thing and one thing only.

'Be silent,' he growled.

Understanding glowed in her eyes, as if she

could see those thorns in his heart. As if she knew how much they hurt and how hard he was fighting them.

She said nothing, only looked at him. And for some reason her silence made him feel even worse, so he jerked her robes up to her waist, uncovering her, not caring if the fabric ripped.

He had to do something to take away the terrible understanding on her lovely face. To strip it from her, turn her pretty eyes dark, make her blind to everything but pleasure. Make her need him.

Prove that you do not need her?

Yes, and that too. Because he didn't. He needed nothing from her but her body.

Under her robes was a pair of loose trousers in the same fine silk, and the material parted without any resistance as he tore them from her, along with the lacy knickers she wore underneath.

She didn't stop him, but he felt her tremble as she was finally bare under his hands, her skin warm and as fine as the silk he'd ripped from her.

His heart was beating so loudly he couldn't

hear a thing, and the edge of hunger inside him was made sharper by the scent of her arousal.

He looked down at the soft, damp nest of curls between her thighs, her skin pink and slick. His hands on her pale flesh looked rough and dark—as if they would tear her as he'd torn the fabric of her robes.

You are unworthy. A disgrace.

He growled again, shoving her thighs wide, wanting to look at her and not listen to his father's voice in his head.

She was so pretty. So delicate. And this was all he needed from her—nothing more. Certainly not friendship. Nothing that would threaten the walls he'd built around himself. Nothing that would threaten his detachment. He was perfectly fine, here in his vacuum.

He slid his hands up her thighs, losing himself in the feel of her beneath his fingertips. Then higher still to the heat that lay between. She sighed as he touched her, parting her wet flesh gently, and the soft, needy sound shivered through him.

Yes, this was how it should be. Her needing him. Her desperate for him. Not the other way around. Never that.

Yet his hands were shaking as he held the soft folds apart, and he was breathing so fast it was as if he couldn't get enough air. And he was ravenous, suffocating in his vacuum, and she was the air he needed to breathe.

He should have stopped then—if only to prove to himself that he could hold himself apart from her. But he couldn't. The hunger was too much to bear.

Leaning forward, he bent his head between her thighs, running his tongue directly up the centre of her sex, desperate for a taste.

She jerked, a soft cry escaping her, but he didn't stop, The hunger was sinking its claws deep into him. He slid his hands to her hips and held her still as he began to explore her, the taste of her exploding in his head, a salty-sweet burst of flavour that made him even harder and more desperate.

'Tariq…' she gasped, twisting in his grip. 'Oh…'

The pleading note in her voice was exactly what he'd been hoping for, so he didn't stop then either, teasing the hard little bud with his tongue and then dipping down, circling the entrance to her body, before pushing inside to taste her deeper.

He wanted her as hungry as he was. As desperate. As frantic. He wanted that terrible knowledge in her eyes gone. She looked at him as if she'd seen inside him and seen the lonely little boy he'd once been. The boy who'd broken under his father's lesson.

The boy who was unworthy, a disgrace to his name.

He would never let himself be that boy again.

She cried out, her fingers tangling in his hair, her grip on him bordering on pain. But that only sharpened everything deliciously, making him growl yet again against her wet flesh and loosen his grip on her hip, sliding his hand beneath the soft curve of her buttocks. Then he tilted her so he could taste her even deeper, making her groan and arch in his hold.

A dark satisfaction at the sound of her cries unwound inside him, along with a deep possessiveness that he couldn't hold back. He would make her forget all this friendship nonsense. Make her forget so completely she'd never think of it again. Yes, and he'd make her forget that her father hadn't wanted her, that her mother hadn't fought for her. He'd make her forget about everything but him and what he could give her. She wouldn't need anything else and neither would he.

He pushed deeper with his tongue and she writhed, her body trembling harder as he brought her to the brink. And then he pushed her over with another wicked lick, holding her tightly as she sobbed and twisted between his hands, the climax riding her hard.

Her scent was all around him, her taste on his tongue, her heat so close, and abruptly his own need tightened its grip around his throat, threatening to choke him.

He let her go, pushing himself back from her. She made a glorious picture, leaning against the back of the couch with her face a deep rosy colour, her eyes glittering and dark with the after-effects of pleasure. Her legs were spread wide, there was the sheen of moisture on her inner thighs, and her sex was open and wet and ready for him.

He reached for the rest of her robes, pulling them away from her until she was sitting there naked, surrounded by blue silk, like a jewel in the middle of fine tissue paper.

'Lie down,' he ordered hoarsely, and rose to

his feet, not taking his gaze from her as she did as she was told, lying back on the couch, naked and beautiful and ready for him.

He couldn't wait to undress. He simply undid his trousers and freed himself, then joined her on the couch, settling himself between her spread thighs. She reached for him but he pushed her hands away, guiding himself to the entrance of her body and thrusting home.

Charlotte gasped and arched beneath him, her silky thighs closing around his hips, her breasts lifting. Her silvery lashes came down, lying on her cheeks, her mouth was slightly open. For a second he couldn't move. Could only gaze down at her beneath him, the grip of her sex around him and the heat of her body blanking his mind utterly.

And it should have been enough. It shouldn't have made him feel so hollow, as if there was something more. Something so close he could almost touch it.

'Look at me,' he demanded roughly, before he could stop himself. 'Look at me, Charlotte.'

Her lashes lifted at his command, her gaze meeting his, and a hot, intense electrical charge pulsed straight through him. For a moment it felt as if he held something in his hands, something ineffable and beautiful, that would break if he gripped it too hard.

There was tenderness in Charlotte's eyes, a warmth that had nothing to do with sexual heat, and she put out a hand, cupping his cheek as if he was the precious thing, the thing that might break.

His chest ached, a heavy weight pressing on it. The consequences of the vacuum in which he'd been trying to breathe for so long. The vacuum that seemed to be suffocating him, after all.

Yet not when she touched him. The contact of her fingers on his cheek, the clutch of her sex around his, the heat of her body and the warmth in her silver-blue eyes were all lifelines containing oxygen.

It felt as if they were the only things keeping him alive.

He took a shaken breath, then another, and when her fingers trailed along his jaw the pressure on his chest lifted. He took another breath, right down deep into his lungs, and it felt like the first breath he'd ever taken.

And when he moved inside her, deep and slow,

it felt as if the pleasure was another lifeline too, another strand connecting him to her.

Her lovely mouth curved, her darkening gaze holding him as fast as the grip of her sex around his shaft, and he couldn't look away.

She could see him. She could see who he was deep down inside. She could see that lonely little boy and she was reaching out a hand to him. She was pulling away the barriers around his heart as if they were nothing but paper. Putting out her hands and holding him.

Holding him as if he was worth something.

He couldn't stop her. Couldn't stop himself from wanting that touch, craving the way she held him, reaching to grasp all the lifelines she was throwing him.

He moved faster, harder, holding on tight to her as he drove into her, their shared breathing fast and ragged in the room. And her hands were on him, stroking him lightly and easily as he drove her down into the cushions. As he felt the pleasure beginning to take him apart.

'Charlotte…' He hadn't meant to say her name—not like that. Not so deep and dark and desperate. 'Little one…'

Her arms were coming around him, her thighs

tightening, embracing him in a way no one had ever held him before. The immensity of his hunger was a tidal wave of need washing up inside him, all the years he'd spent alone crashing down on him.

But he wasn't alone. Not now. Because now he had her. She was his wife and she could never leave. She was safe.

The thought stayed with him as he tore her hands from his body and pushed them up and behind her head, holding them down with his own. And it glowed brightly as he thrust harder into her, the couch shaking with the force of it, burying all the heat and desperation inside her with every flex of his hips.

And she met every thrust, panting and as wild as he was, his name on her lips as she arched and moved beneath him, the pleasure becoming more intense, more raw with every movement.

It was too much to look at her. The wild blue of her eyes ripped him apart. And he only had time to shove his hand between them, stroking her sex hard and sure, feeling the wave of her climax hit as she convulsed beneath him.

Then he was following her, his own hitting

him, stealing every breath from his body and every thought from his head.

Minutes or maybe hours later, the feel of her hands drifting down his back returned him to himself and he tried to shift his weight off her. But she made a little protesting sound, her nails digging into his hips, clearly wanting him to stay where he was. So he did, propping himself up on his elbows instead and looking down at her.

She didn't speak, and neither did he, and for long moments he simply let himself be lost in the endless blue of her eyes.

'My father wanted to disown me when he found out what I had told Catherine,' he heard himself say, giving her the final piece of himself—the piece he'd told no one else about. 'He called me a disgrace...said I was unworthy.'

There was tenderness in her eyes, and sympathy too. 'Your father was wrong about a lot of things, Tariq. And most especially that.'

He wanted to disagree with her, but that was a question for another day. Right now there were more important things to do. Like picking her up and carrying her to his bed. And then maybe, after they had sated themselves again, they could even have a conversation.

'I am not letting you leave, *ya amar*,' he said. 'You understand that, do you not? You are mine.'

Something in her face relaxed—a tightness he hadn't noticed before. 'I know. You've said that before, believe it or not.'

'I am not joking.'

One fair brow rose. 'Were you joking before?'

'Let us just say that I did not know that I was in a vacuum.' He paused, holding her gaze. 'And that I needed air in order to breathe.'

CHAPTER ELEVEN

CHARLOTTE WAS IN the middle of yet more language lessons with Amirah when one of the palace servants knocked on the door of her suite, issuing a summons to Tariq's study.

It had been a week since he'd taken her in the library, when it had felt as if the earth had shifted beneath her and something had changed between them. She hadn't been able to stop thinking about how he'd said he needed air to breathe, and had looked at her intently, as if *she* was the air. He hadn't said it outright, but she'd felt it. As if he'd finally discovered the connection that had been forged between them back in the oasis.

He was such a lonely man—a man desperate for someone—and she'd tasted desperation in his kiss. Felt it in the way he'd taken her. It had made her heart twist in her chest, made her want to give whatever she could, coax his rare and beautiful smile from him. Make him laugh.

Take the loneliness from him and give him comfort instead.

So she'd spent time over the past week doing things with him that weren't based either around sex or his duties as ruler. Things that friends did together. A relaxed dinner by the fountains, talking about nothing in particular. Watching a movie in the palace's own cinema. An outing into the city, where he'd shown her a few of his favourite places. A horse ride into the southern hills.

They had been special moments. When he hadn't been the king and she hadn't been his queen. When they'd simply been Tariq and Charlotte, enjoying each other's company.

She didn't know why she wanted to do this for the man who was keeping her from her family and friends and who'd pretty much forced her to marry him. But she didn't let herself think too deeply about it. Being with him made her feel less lonely, and that was enough. In fact, for the first time in her life she felt wanted—and not only that but needed too. Needed by a king.

That fact alone had given her a courage and strength she'd never known possible.

After the summons arrived she let Amirah

go for the rest of the day, then made her way through the palace corridors to Tariq's study.

He was sitting behind his vast desk as she came in and closed the door behind her, glancing up from his computer screen as she approached.

This past week she'd been the lucky recipient of quite a few of his smiles, but not today. His expression remained grim and a sense of foreboding stole through her, making her feel cold. Then he stood and came around the side of the desk, and abruptly she felt even colder.

'What is it?' she asked as he approached.

'I've just had word that your father had a heart attack last night and has been taken to hospital.' His voice was level and matter-of-fact as he stopped in front of her, reaching for her hands and taking them in his own.

Shock echoed through her. 'I don't…' She tried to get her brain working. 'Dad's in hospital?'

Tariq's fingers were warm as they wrapped around hers, and when he drew her to him she didn't resist, needing the strength of his tall, muscular body, because suddenly she was afraid she might fall.

'Yes.' His deep voice calmed her somewhat. 'As I said, he had a heart attack.'

'How bad is it?'

'They're not sure. I spoke to your father's doctor myself, and it appears that it may take some time to see how severe the damage is. But it's entirely possible that he'll make a full recovery.'

Charlotte swallowed. Tariq's warmth surrounded her, and the heat of his skin burning against her numb fingers comforted her.

Her father wasn't perfect, but he was her father all the same, and although he hadn't exactly made her feel wanted, he *had* taken care of her after her mother had left. He'd fed and clothed her, given her a roof over her head and ensured she'd got a decent education. He'd never been actively cruel or abused her. But now he was sick. Now he was alone…

She couldn't bear the thought of that. He might not be the world's greatest dad, but that didn't mean she could leave him in hospital with no support. He had no other family except her. Besides, she wasn't like her mother—she couldn't simply walk away when someone needed her.

Charlotte lifted her head and stared up into the hard gold of her husband's eyes. 'I have to go to him. I have to go back to England.'

There was sympathy in Tariq's expression, but

his voice when he spoke was firm. 'The borders are closed, *ya amar*. You may not leave.'

'This is different. Dad's ill.'

Yet he only shook his head. 'It does not matter. I cannot let you go.'

'Why not?' She frowned, not understanding. 'Surely this is allowed? He's sick. And there's no one else to take care of him.'

The planes and angles of Tariq's fiercely beautiful face hardened, the warmth that had been there before fading. 'That is what a hospital full of doctor and nurses is for, is it not?'

'But…he's my father, Tariq. And it won't be for long, I promise.' She squeezed his hand in reassurance. 'I'll just see that he's okay and then—'

'No.' Tariq's voice was flat, and all sympathy drained abruptly from his expression.

She blinked at his tone, instinctive anger licking up inside her, and opened her mouth to tell him he was being unreasonable.

Then she caught a glint of what looked like fear in his golden eyes.

Her anger disappeared as quickly as it had risen.

'What's wrong?' she asked quietly, because it

was clear something was. 'This isn't just about Dad, is it?'

His features had turned forbidding, as if she'd seen something he didn't want her to see.

'You are my sheikha. You cannot simply leave the country whenever the mood takes you.'

'This is not a "mood", Tariq.'

The glint in his eyes blazed unexpectedly, his grip on her hand tightening. 'I do not care. You are my sheikha and your place is by my side.'

Her heart clenched at the intensity in his face and the fierce note in his voice. At how much he needed her. And part of her didn't want to push him or argue, because she liked it that he did.

But this was important to her. And, anyway, she would come back. It wasn't as if she was going for good.

'I know,' she said, trying to sound calm. 'But it won't be for long, I promise. Only until I know what's happening with Dad and then I'll be back.'

The ferocity in Tariq's expression didn't lessen. 'You have no idea how long it will be. And what if he needs long-term care? What if he is hospitalised for good? What will you do then?'

'I'll work something out. It won't be an issue.'

She reached up to touch his cheek, wanting to soothe him. 'Please don't—'

But he didn't wait for her to finish, releasing her all of a sudden and turning away so that she touched nothing but empty air.

Charlotte stared after him as he stalked back to his desk, her heart beating faster. Something was wrong and she didn't know what it was.

'What is it?' she asked into the tense silence. 'You know I'll come back. I will, Tariq. I promise.'

He was standing with his back to her, looking out over the gardens through the window, the line of his powerful shoulders stiff with tension. 'I have been promised things before. Promises mean nothing.'

'But, I can—'

'No.' He turned sharply, pinning her with that fierce, hot stare. 'If I let you go, what will bring you back? Me?'

She stared at him, bewildered. 'Of course. You're my husband.'

'A man you were forced into marrying. A husband who keeps you here against your will.'

'Yes, you've done those things, but it's different now. I said I'd stay and I meant it. I'm your wife, not to mention your friend. I would never walk out on you.'

'No,' he said flatly. 'I cannot risk it.'

'Tariq—'

'My father kept everything that was good from me when I was growing up and I told myself that I did not need it. But you have made me see things differently, Charlotte. This week you have made me see what I have been missing. You have made me see what I need. And now I have that I do not want to give it up.' Fire burned in his eyes, a deep, fierce amber. 'I told you that you were mine and so you are. And I do not give up what is mine. I will not.'

He *was* afraid—she could see it in his eyes. He was afraid she wouldn't return.

'You can trust me,' she said, trying to calm him. 'I give you my word.'

Anger flashed across his intense features. 'Do you think that I am a skittish horse that needs soothing? I have been lied to before, so do not think that your "word" will work.'

Of course. Catherine and her promises to him. But, no, this went deeper than Catherine. This was about his father. This was about himself.

Automatically, she opened her mouth to say

something that would ease his anger, and then stopped.

Why? Why are you always placating him? When you know he's being unreasonable?

That was a very good question. And it was a question she didn't have the answer to. But, no, that was wrong. She did have the answer. She just didn't want to acknowledge it. She wanted to pretend it didn't exist.

Except it did exist.

It was staring her in the face and had been for weeks.

She always wanted to soothe him and comfort him because he mattered to her. Because she loved him. She'd been in love with him since the moment he'd taken her in that tent at the oasis.

Charlotte's chest tightened as the knowledge swept through her, overwhelming her, making it hard to breathe, making her feel dizzy.

Her mouth was as dry as the desert and she was afraid. Because she knew all about love. Love was pain. Love was listening to her parents scream at each other over her head. Love was watching her mother give up on her and walk away. Love was the ache that cut deep inside every time her father looked at her as if she was nothing but a nuisance to him.

Love was giving everything and getting nothing in return.

She stared at her handsome husband, her heart roaring in her ears. Stared at the man to whom she was slowly, little by little, giving away the pieces of her soul. And he was taking it. He was keeping it for himself and giving her nothing back.

And you've done that before, haven't you?

Of course she had. With her father. Being quiet and good for him…not causing a fuss as a child. Helping him with his career and being his dogsbody as an adult. Trying and trying to get him to look at her with something more than impatience and frustration. To see her as his daughter and not the millstone around his neck that she suspected he thought she was.

You tried to make him to care. But he never did. And now you're doing the same with Tariq.

'You're very clear about what you want,' she said suddenly, hoarsely. 'But what about what I want? Does that not matter at all?'

His expression was hard. Cold. The mask of the sheikh.

'What has that got to do with anything?'

'Answer the question.'

Something flickered across his face and then it was gone. 'That is not a requirement.'

An empty, hollow feeling opened inside her. He didn't care what she wanted, which meant he didn't care about her.

Did you expect that he would?

Maybe she'd hoped. Maybe that was why she'd never looked too closely at her own feelings. Because she knew she wouldn't be able to bear the disappointment if he didn't feel the same way. But he'd told her in the tent at the oasis that theirs would only be a physical marriage, and she'd been okay with it back then. She hadn't expected or wanted more.

Except things had changed. He'd given her physical pleasure, made her feel beautiful, and then, over the past week together, he'd given her his friendship. He'd made her feel interesting and special. Desirable, sexy and brave. He'd made her feel needed.

And that was the problem.

He'd made her want more.

He'd made her want to be loved.

'It's a requirement for me,' she said, her voice cracking.

And just like that the fierce expression on his face closed, like the door of a furnace shutting, depriving her of all its light and all its heat.

'In that case perhaps you are not as suited to life here as I expected.'

His voice was hard as stone, his gaze as pitiless as it had been that day she'd fainted in front of him.

'Perhaps it would be better if you returned to England, after all.'

Somewhere deep inside her she felt a tearing pain.

So much for all your hopes. If he can give you up so easily, then he really doesn't care.

He stood on the other side of the desk and the distance between them felt vast, cavernous. He was so isolated, and so lonely, and there was a part of her that wanted more than anything to bridge that gap.

But she wasn't the same woman she'd been a couple of weeks ago. She'd found a strength inside her she hadn't thought possible. And she was tired of giving everything of herself to someone who would never give anything back. She didn't want to do it any more.

So if he expected her to soothe and placate him, to beg him to let her stay, he was in for a surprise. Because she wasn't going to. She wasn't going to demand he tell her why he'd changed his mind either. If he wanted to sit here in splendid isolation, in his arid life in a vacuum, then he could.

She wouldn't stop him, not this time.

Charlotte drew herself up, looking him in the eye even as her heart shredded itself in her chest. 'Fine,' she said. 'Then you can arrange for me to fly out tonight.'

A fleeting look of shock crossed his face before it was quickly masked. 'Charlotte—'

'No,' she interrupted, furious and heartbroken, everything hot and raw. 'You will damn well listen to what I have to say. I'm not choosing to leave because I want to. I'm choosing to leave because you haven't given me one single reason to stay.'

She found she was shaking.

'You made it clear what our marriage was. Right from the beginning you told me, and I thought I was okay with it. I thought I didn't want more. But I've changed my mind.'

She met his gaze head-on.

'I've decided I do want more. I want a real marriage, Tariq, emotional as well as physical. I want love. Give me that and I swear no power on earth will make me leave you.'

He was suddenly still, as if she'd turned him to stone. And the silence deepened, lengthened.

'I cannot,' he said at last, roughly, as if it had been dragged from him. 'That is the one thing I cannot give you.'

It wasn't a shock. It wasn't even a surprise. And maybe that was what hurt most of all. She knew he couldn't. And whether it was a case of him not being able to or simply not wanting to, it didn't matter.

The outcome was still the same.

Charlotte ignored the desert that had taken the place of her heart. She didn't plead with him, didn't beg. Didn't ask him why. All she said was, 'Then I have to leave.'

The mask of the sheikh had settled back over his strong features once again, and there was no emotion at all in his eyes. 'I will have Faisal handle your travel arrangements,' he said, without any discernible emotion. 'You will, of course, let me know if you discover you are pregnant.'

That hurt—as he must have known it would.

But she didn't let it show.

She turned on her heel and left him there.

Tariq stood in front of the window for a long time after she'd gone, staring out at his beautiful gardens and the fountains playing, desperate for the peaceful scene to calm the sudden and terrible rage that clawed up inside him. Desperate to find his detachment, the black silence of his vacuum.

But it was nowhere to be found, so he stayed where he was, unmoving. Because if he moved even a muscle he wasn't sure that he wouldn't go running after Charlotte, pick her up and toss her over his shoulder, carry her into his bedroom, lock the door, throw away the key.

He couldn't do that, though. No matter how much he wanted to. No matter how much the pain in her silver-blue eyes had felt like glass sliding under his skin. Or how her request for love had made that glass slice through his soul. Or how her leaving had made him feel suffocated, left to bear the crushing weight of his isolation alone.

No, he couldn't go after her. Couldn't give her the one thing—the only thing—she'd ever asked of him.

He couldn't give her love.

He'd worked too hard, borne too much, to give in to those terrible betraying feelings. Being true to his father's teachings, keeping himself isolated—that was all he could do now. And if he felt as if he was dying inside, then that was his own fault. He'd been the one to think he could have friendship and pleasure, that he could have her smile and her laughter—all the things he'd been missing in his life and all without consequence.

Little by little she'd got past his walls and he should have stopped her days ago. He'd let her get too far and this was the result: his detachment, the thing he needed to be a good king, cracked and broken.

'Does what I want not matter at all?'

Tariq stared sightlessly at the fountain, her voice and the break in it replaying in his head. He'd told her that she was his, that he would never let her go, but the moment she'd said those words and he'd felt something inside him twist and crack he'd understood.

She had to leave. She made him feel too much. She made him *feel*, full stop. And that was a very bad thing. It compromised the very foundation he'd built his life upon, not to mention his reign, and that he wouldn't allow. He couldn't put himself and what he wanted first because he was responsible for an entire nation. And keeping it safe was his primary objective.

Even if that meant keeping it safe from himself.

He'd put his country at risk once before because he'd been too much a slave to his emotions. He couldn't do it again.

'I want love, Tariq. Give me that.'

No, not even for her.

It was a long time before he permitted himself to move. A long time before he turned away from the window, forcing himself to make a few calls, arranging the travel details for her himself.

Then, once that was done, he shut himself in his office, leaving instructions with his guards that he was not to be disturbed under any circumstances.

And he threw himself into work.

* * *

A week later and he still hadn't granted anyone an audience or interview. He'd refused meetings. Even requests for casual conversation had been ignored.

Everyone had been turned away from his door.

He didn't want to see anyone. He didn't want to talk to anyone.

He had to shore up the cracks in his armour that Charlotte had created and he could only do that alone.

The week turned into two and then three.

Faisal came at least once every day, demanding admittance, but Tariq ignored him.

Yet he still couldn't find any peace.

One evening he headed to the palace baths, as he had every night since Charlotte had left, unable to sleep and tortured by a warmth that wasn't there. By memories of soft curves and hair like moonlight. Of deep blue eyes that had looked at him as if there was something worthy in him when he knew there wasn't.

He flung himself into the water, driving his hands through it as if he was digging himself out of a hole, or pulling himself up a sharp cliff, swimming on and on. Driving himself into the spurious peace of exhaustion.

That exhaustion never lasted, though, and once it had passed the ache would return, bringing with it the intense longing and the sense of suffocation. As if the air he needed to breathe was being depleted and he was slowly choking and by inches dying.

You need air. You need her.

He forced that thought from his head, driving himself harder through the water.

No, he'd been fine before she came to him and he would be fine again. All he needed to do was hold fast to his detachment and these sensations would pass. They had after Catherine and they would again—he was sure of it.

His hand hit the end of the pool again, but this time, sensing someone standing there, he stopped and stood up, pushing his hair back from his eyes.

Faisal stood at the edge, his expression impassive.

'How did you get past the guards?' Tariq demanded gracelessly. His temper these days was on a hair trigger. 'No one is permitted to enter.'

'I knocked them out.' Faisal's tone was short. 'You need new guards.'

Tariq scowled. He didn't want Faisal here. He didn't want to talk. He wanted to continue swimming until his muscles ached and he was exhausted, the feeling of being suffocated gone.

'What do you want?' he asked. 'Tell me, then get out.'

Faisal stared at him a moment, then said with unexpected savagery, 'You're a fool, Tariq. Sulking in your palace alone. Why did you send her away?'

Tariq felt his hands clench into fists and he had to force the anger away, get himself under control. 'I do not recall asking for your opinion, Faisal. And be careful what you say—'

'Your father was a fool too,' the old man interrupted harshly. 'He closed himself down completely after your mother died—did you know that? He never got over it. He isolated himself and then he did the same to you.'

Tariq went still.

'I told him it was wrong,' Faisal went on. 'That just because he had lost his wife it did not mean that his son should not find happiness and companionship. But he ignored me. And now look what has happened.' The old advisor virtually spat the words. 'You have closed the borders of your country and your heart. You are him in everything but name.'

Abruptly the weight sitting on Tariq's chest increased, like a vice crushing him, the vacuum pressing in. He should command Faisal's silence, tell him to get out, but he couldn't speak.

'Do you know what happens to a tree with its roots cut?' Faisal asked, suddenly quiet. 'Or to a fire starved of oxygen? It dies.' There was a pause. 'Your insistence on your father's outdated lessons may not end up killing this country, Tariq. But it will certainly end up killing you.'

The water was cool, but suddenly he was burning up. The emotions inside him, the anger and desperation and longing, were too strong and too powerful. They were inescapable and there was nowhere for them to go but inward. And now they were eating him alive.

'Perhaps,' he heard himself say roughly, 'that should have happened years ago. Before I betrayed Ashkaraz in a rush of foolish temper.'

Faisal was silent, but Tariq couldn't look at

him. He couldn't bear to see what was on the old man's face.

'No,' Faisal said at last. 'No, that is not true. It was your father who betrayed Ashkaraz. If he had brought you up with love, rather than harshness, you would not have been so lonely. And if you had not been so lonely you would not have been angry with him. You would not have turned to Catherine.'

'You cannot say that—'

'I can and I will,' the old man interrupted. 'You are a good king, Tariq. But you could be a great one. Better than your father ever was. Because you have what he lacked: a strong and passionate heart. You just need to use it.'

His jaw ached, along with every muscle in his body. He felt as if he was standing on the edge of a cliff, the ledge crumbling beneath him. 'Detachment is what makes a great king, Faisal. Not a strong and passionate heart.'

'That is your father talking.' Faisal's voice was uncompromising. 'And he was wrong. Love is what makes a great king.'

A few weeks ago he would have ignored the words. Now they settled into him, through the chink in his armour that Charlotte had left there.

He didn't know how long he stood in the chilly waters of the baths after Faisal had gone, watching the light filter down from the hidden windows in the ceiling, his heart beating fast and getting faster, the emotions inside him burning him alive.

If love was what made a great king, then that was something he couldn't be. Because what did he know of love? It was his father's grief and pain. It was Catherine's empty promises. His own anger and betrayal…

That's not all it is.

He caught his breath, memories coiling through him. Charlotte's gentle hand on his skin. Charlotte's smile as she looked up at him. Charlotte's arms around him, holding him close.

'I want love,' she'd said—as if she knew exactly what it was, as if it was something to be deeply desired and longed for and not something that led to pain and betrayal.

Faisal isn't wrong. If your father had even let you have one friend, one connection, would you have gone to Catherine that night?

Perhaps he wouldn't. Perhaps he wouldn't have been so lonely and so angry. So desperate for any connection that he'd let his father's mistress seduce him. Perhaps if his father had brought him up with love he'd understand what Charlotte wanted.

You can understand now.

The thought made air rush abruptly into his lungs and he found himself gasping, as if he'd forgotten how to breathe.

'You have what he lacked...' Faisal had said. *'A strong and passionate heart. You just need to use it.'*

And to do that he needed to open it. To stop fighting his emotions. To embrace them, make them part of him.

So he did. He stood in the water, his hands in fists, his skin getting cold, and instead of fighting the feelings inside him he set them free, let them rush through him like oxygen down an air line.

And suddenly everything became clear.

He loved Charlotte Devereaux.

He'd loved her for weeks.

She made him better. She made him stronger. She made him compassionate and merciful and protective. She made him humble.

She made him whole.

She made him the king he should be for his people.

And if he wanted to be that king he needed her at his side.

Give her a reason to be there, then.

His heart was beating far too fast and his hands were shaking—because there was only one thing he could offer her and that was himself, and he was honest enough to admit that probably wasn't enough. She'd told him she'd wanted love from him, but maybe after the way she'd left, after the way he'd treated her, she had changed her mind.

But he had to go to her and offer it anyway. He needed to show her that what she wanted mattered to him. He needed to tell her that she was loved. That she was his queen, and to death and beyond would remain so.

Tariq moved to the edge of the pool and hauled himself out. It was late, and he should go to bed, but he wasn't tired. Instead he dried himself off and went straight to his office.

He worked through the night, putting various and very necessary things in motion. And then, just as dawn was breaking, he finally put through the call he'd been waiting all night to make.

'Ready my jet,' he ordered, when one of his assistants answered. 'I will be flying to London as soon as possible.'

CHAPTER TWELVE

CHARLOTTE SMOOTHED THE blanket over her father's knees as he sat in his favourite armchair beside the fire in the living room and ignored his fussing. Luckily the heart attack had been mild, and the doctor was incredibly pleased with his progress—but he was a terrible patient. He wanted to be back in his office at the university, putting together a new lecture or organising a new dig, not sitting 'mouldering' at home. At least, that was what he kept saying to her, as if he was expecting her to do something about it.

'I don't have my laptop,' he said peevishly, readjusting the blanket. 'How am I supposed to prepare anything when I don't have my laptop? I need you to go into my office and get—'

'No, Dad.' Charlotte interrupted, before he could get into a list of all the things he needed. 'I have a job interview tomorrow, so you'll have to wait.'

It was for an office job, doing administrative

tasks, and she'd been surprised she'd got an interview, given her lack of work experience. But she'd felt a vague sense of satisfaction that she'd managed to score it. Now her father was better, and would be returning to work in the next week or so, her own life could resume. Not that she knew quite what that life was going to look like.

One thing was clear, though: it wasn't going to be what she'd had before.

When she'd come back to England she'd been caught up in her father's illness and looking after him, too busy to think about what her next move might be. But since he'd been released from hospital, and she'd had to move into her father's mews house in order to look after him, she'd had time to make a few decisions. And one of those was that she wasn't going to be returning to work for him.

She was done with men who did nothing but take.

She was going to do what *she* wanted for a change.

'You don't need a job.' He fussed with his blanket yet again. 'You can be my assistant. The new one isn't working out as well as I'd hoped.'

Once upon a time Charlotte might have leapt at the opportunity. But not now.

Not since Tariq.

The thought of the man she'd left behind made the wound deep inside her soul ache, but she shoved the pain away. She'd made her choice and she didn't regret it. And if sometimes at night, when she couldn't sleep, she wished she'd confronted him when he'd told her he couldn't give her love, then what of it? It didn't change what had happened, and it was far too late to confront him now anyway.

The borders of Ashkaraz were closed to her and so was its sheikh's heart.

'Thanks, Dad, but, no,' Charlotte said firmly. 'It's time I started living my own life, making my own choices.'

Her father scowled. 'The new girl doesn't do things the way I like them.'

'Then I'm afraid that's your problem, not mine.'

'Charlotte…'

'What?' She gave him a very direct look. 'I'm your daughter, not your servant. Not your dogsbody. Not any more. I have things *I* want to do.'

He was silent a moment. Then, 'You've changed. What happened in Ashkaraz?'

It was the first time he'd asked her, and Charlotte debated for a moment whether or not he deserved an explanation. But perhaps it would be good for him to hear a few home truths.

'I had my heart broken,' she said flatly. 'And I realised that for years I've been trying to prove myself to a man who took what I had to give him and never saw me as anything more than a nuisance. And even though I gave up a piece of my soul to come back and help him recover, he hasn't even said thank you. Not once. Is that enough of an explanation for you?'

Her father at least had the grace to look ashamed of himself.

There was a long, uncomfortable silence. Then he said, 'I'm sorry. I know I haven't been the… best of fathers. But, well… You look at lot like her. Your mother, I mean. And sometimes I forget that you're not her.'

Charlotte's throat closed. He'd never talked to her like this.

'It was never about you,' he added gruffly. 'You were a good girl. A good daughter. And I…missed you while you were gone.'

It was as close as her father would ever come to an explanation for his behaviour, and maybe an apology as well. But she didn't need his approval to make her feel good about herself—not these days—so all she said was, 'Good. I'm glad you did.'

He didn't say much after that, and a bit later, discovering that there was no milk for their tea, Charlotte decided that she'd have to brave the rain in order to get some.

She grabbed an umbrella from the stand in the hallway and headed out.

The cobbles in the mews outside her father's house were shiny and slippery, and it was cold. And as the hand clutching the handle of the umbrella went numb Charlotte found herself wishing she was somewhere hot. Where the sun was merciless and the sand was burning. Where neither were as hot as the passion of the man she'd left there.

Her heart squeezed and she had to grit her teeth against a wave of pain. Why was she thinking of Tariq again? Leaving had been the right thing to do. The *only* thing. Thinking of him hurt. Besides, she'd find herself someone else. He wasn't the only fish in the sea.

Except you will never love anyone as you loved him.

The thought was so bleak that she had to stop, because her vision was swimming with tears and it hurt to breathe. Then, as she collected herself and prepared to go on, she noticed someone standing in the mews ahead of her.

And everything in her went quiet and still.

It was a very tall man and he was holding a black umbrella. He was dressed in what looked like a shockingly expensive dark suit, with sunglasses over his eyes despite the rain. But even the suit and the glasses couldn't disguise the sense of authority and arrogance he radiated.

Except Charlotte didn't need that to know who it was.

She would have known him anywhere.

Tariq.

Her poor, shattered heart seized in her chest and she blinked—because surely he wasn't here. This had to be a mirage. Yet despite the blinking he didn't disappear, and, yes, it seemed that he really was here, in London. Standing in the road near her father's house.

Then he was coming towards her, moving with the same fluid grace she remembered, and just like that rage filled her, making her shake.

How dared he come here? After she'd made

the horrifically painful decision to leave him. After her heart had torn itself to pieces as she'd walked away. After she'd wept all the way back to London and for days afterwards, missing him so acutely it had felt like being stabbed.

After all that he'd come here. Why? What did he want from her? Was it to hurt her again? Taunt her with what she could never have?

Charlotte didn't wait for him to reach her. She stormed up to him instead, meeting him in the middle of the lane. Then she reached up and tore the glasses from his face so she could see him, holding the familiar intensity of his golden stare with her own.

He didn't move. Didn't speak. Only stared at her.

'What are you doing here?' she demanded, her voice breaking, even though she tried not to let it. 'How dare you? How dare you come here to—?'

It was only then that he moved, throwing away his umbrella as if he didn't care about the rain that was falling around them and stepping under hers. Then he reached for her, taking her face between his hands, and the warmth of his skin was like a bolt of lightning, rooting her to the spot.

He bent and kissed her, his mouth hot and desperate, and the taste of him was so achingly familiar that tears rushed into her eyes, the deep hunger inside her stirring, waking.

Oh, God, how could he do this to her?

She stiffened, ready to push him away, but he'd already lifted his head, the look in his eyes blazing.

'Oh, *ya amar*,' he said fiercely. 'I have been such a fool. I have done such stupid things. Said things I should not have. And all I can say is that I am sorry.' His thumbs moved caressingly over her cheekbones. 'I should have let you go to your father. I should have trusted you to return. And most important of all I should have given you a reason to come back to me.'

She was trembling and unable to stop. Unable to pull away from him either. All she could do was stand there and look up into the blazing gold of his eyes.

'What reason?' she asked, trying to hold herself together.

The lines of his beautiful face took on a familiar intensity. 'You asked me to give you love. So I am here to offer it.'

Her umbrella didn't protect him from the rain and his black hair was getting wet, his suit damp, water was trickling down the side of his face. But he didn't seem to notice. His attention was on her as if he was suffocating and she was the lifeline he needed.

Except it was she who couldn't breathe.

'Be clear, Tariq.' She barely sounded like herself. 'What are you saying?'

'I am saying that I love you, Charlotte Devereaux,' Tariq said in his dark, deep voice. 'I love you, my wife. I have spent the past three weeks telling myself that sending you away would stop these feelings inside me. That once you were gone I could stay detached. Be the kind of king my father wanted me to be. But I could not do it. I could not escape what I feel for you. And I found out that...*you* are what makes me the king I need to be.'

His gaze searched her face, unhidden desperation in it.

'You make me compassionate and merciful. You make me humble. You make me strong. You make me a better man, a better king. And I want to give you back everything that you have given me.'

She felt cold, and then hot, as if she was dying and then coming back to life. 'Tariq...'

His name was the only thing she could say.

Luckily she didn't need to speak, because he went on, 'I want you, *ya amar*. I want to give you all the love you need. And I would leave Ashkaraz if I could, be with you here in London if you wanted me to. But I cannot leave my country. So all I can do is beg you to return with me.'

Her heart felt both heavy and light at the same time, at the ferocity in his eyes, at his desperation and his anguish.

She looked up at him, drinking in every line of his beloved face. 'Then I will,' she said simply. Because this was what she'd been wanting her entire life.

And something blazed in his beautiful eyes—heat like the sun, burning there. 'You would do that? After everything that I did to you? Kept you prisoner...made you marry me? Gave you ultimatum after ultimatum—?'

Charlotte reached out and put a shaking finger on his mouth, silencing him. 'After you gave me pleasure and friendship. Showed me how brave I could be and how strong. After you helped me figure out my own worth.' She pressed harder, feeling the heat of his skin beneath her fingertip. 'Yes, you fool. Of course I would do that.'

'I am not a good man, *ya amar.* And there is much I do not understand. I will make mistakes and I will need you to help me. I am also very possessive of what is mine, and that might be… annoying for you. Are you sure you want to commit yourself to that?'

She blinked back sudden tears, her throat aching with an intense joy. 'I've had some experience of dealing with difficult men, believe me. I think I can handle it.'

His expression turned even fiercer. 'Then you have my word that I will do everything in my power to make you happy for the rest of our lives.'

There was rain on her cheeks, though some of the moisture might have been tears, because the iron band that had been around her heart since she'd left him burst open and her chest filled, her lungs filled. Her heart filled.

And then her umbrella was on the ground too, and she was in his arms. His mouth was on hers, tasting of rain and heat and the volcanic passion that was part of him.

'Tell me,' he said roughly when she finally pulled away.

'Tell you what? About my dad?' God, how she

loved to tease him. 'About the job interview I have tomorrow?'

'No.' That dark intensity was back in his face. 'Do not play with me, *ya amar.*'

Charlotte relented. 'You mean tell you that I love you?'

'Yes,' he said fiercely. 'That.'

'Well, I do. I love you. And I—'

He kissed her yet again, hard, cutting off the words, stealing all her breath and then giving it back to her, so that when he raised his head again, she felt light-headed and dizzy.

'I have a hotel nearby,' he murmured. 'Come with me, wife. I need you.'

'Wait.' She pressed her hands to his hard chest, warm despite the fact that they were both soaking wet. 'You need to tell me what changed your mind.'

And, wonderfully, a fleeting magical smile crossed his face. 'A friend.'

She stared at him in surprise. 'I thought you didn't have any?'

'Turns out I have one at least. Faisal. He told me that the reason that my father brought me up the way he did was because he never got over my mother's death. That he cut himself off and did the same to me.' Tariq pushed her damp hair back from her face. 'Faisal also told me that my father was wrong. That it isn't detachment that makes a great king. It's love.' He searched her face. 'I think I am starting to see what he meant. But perhaps you can show me the rest?'

Her heart was bursting, everything she felt for him flooding out. She reached up on tiptoes and kissed him yet again, because all the kisses in the world wouldn't be enough.

'Yes. Yes, I can.'

And she did.

And even though getting lost in the desert might have been the stupidest thing she'd ever done, it had also been the best.

Because in getting lost she'd found her home.

She'd found her for ever.

She'd found herself.

In the strong and passionate heart of a king.

EPILOGUE

THE KNOCK CAME on the door of Tariq's office, and he'd barely had a moment to acknowledge it before it opened and his wife came in.

She was dressed in a deep pink robe today, and it brought a delightful blush to her pale cheeks as well as highlighting her silvery hair.

He smiled, his heartbeat quickening, her presence already brightening his day. 'What is it, *ya amar*?' He pushed back his chair and raised one brow. 'It had better be good. I have a very important report to read.'

'Oh, it is, don't worry.'

She gave him a secretive smile in return, then moved over to his desk and, ignoring the fact that it was the middle of the day and there were other people around, came around it and sat on his lap as if she belonged there.

Which she did.

'This is highly irregular,' he murmured as she settled back against his shoulder and lifted her mouth for his kiss. 'Perhaps we should lock the door?'

Because he was hard and getting harder and—

His thoughts broke off and he went quite still. She was looking at him with a very particular kind of focus.

'Charlotte? What is it?'

Her smile this time was breathtaking. 'What's "Daddy" in Arabic again? I feel our child will want to call you something.'

Everything in him became bright, burning. 'Charlotte...' he said again.

She touched his cheek, and everything he'd ever wanted was right there in her blue eyes.

'Are you going to faint, dear heart?' she asked.

But he didn't faint. He laughed instead, and kissed her, filling himself up with her heat, and her brightness, and all the love she'd brought into his life so far.

And all the love she had yet to bring.

* * * * *

LET'S TALK
Romance

For exclusive extracts, competitions
and special offers, find us online:

f facebook.com/millsandboon

⊙ @millsandboonuk

🐦 @millsandboon

Or get in touch on 0844 844 1351*

For all the latest titles coming soon,
visit millsandboon.co.uk/nextmonth

*Calls cost 7p per minute plus your phone company's price per
minute access charge

Want even more
ROMANCE?

Join our bookclub today!